Storm Clouds
Over Chantel

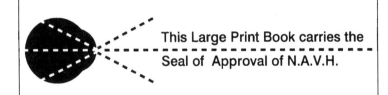

This Large Print Book carries the
Seal of Approval of N.A.V.H.

Storm Clouds Over Chantel

Colleen L. Reece

Walker Large Print • Waterville, Maine

Storm Clouds Over Chantel

PART 1

1

Great June thunderheads rolled above as Chantel Evans crept through the back door and into the yard. Biting her lip at the rasp of the gate, she ran across the small yard, down the alley, and into the cemetery at the end of the street. Straight as a singing bullet, she sped to a far corner, sheltered by a great elm from the curious glances of passersby. She sank to a grasscovered mound, stifled a half-sob, half-laugh. What would her proper Bostonian stepmother and stepsister think of her kneeling by a grave, gowned in a newly finished wedding dress? If anyone reported her to Lydia and Anita — she shuddered. They would never forgive her for making what they would call a "spectacle" of herself.

"I don't care." The firm chin, so unexpected in her delicate face, set in an unaccustomed stubborn line. Her slender figure straightened, and fire came into her eyes, which were as dark as the ebony hair touching the delicate white lace on her shoulders. "It's the only way I can feel close to you, Father." Her slim fingers traced the engraving on the stone.

Charles Evans, Jr.
Born June 4, 1830
Died June 10, 1881
"Asleep in Jesus"

Chantel's mouth twisted. That last line had been cause for a terrible argument within a few days of her father's death. She had kept from crying out against the ostentatious funeral Lydia insisted on having, but when it came to the stone, Chantel was adamant. "He asked for it to be there. He cared more about the Lord Jesus in the last few years than anything. He wanted it as a witness."

"A witness to what a fanatic he turned out to be!" Every highly coiffed curl of Lydia's blond hair registered indignation.

The family solicitor intervened. "It's what he instructed in his papers, Mrs. Evans."

Lydia gave in with bad grace, pulling her eighteen-year-old daughter, Anita, a replica of herself, from the room. "Very well. Just don't expect us to visit the grave."

As far as Chantel knew, in the year since

Father had died, neither Lydia nor Anita had ever been there. In her secret heart she was glad. To have had them there would somehow have desecrated the hallowed spot. Although they had observed the full year's mourning period, their lives were far from mournful. Only the expensive black outfits they wore paid token tribute to the passing of the kindly man who had married Lydia when Chantel was small and even insisted on legally adopting Anita and giving her the Evans name.

Chantel shivered in the growing wind and pulled her cobwebby gown closer. What a long year it had been! As if freed from restraint, the woman who had at least tolerated her changed to the wicked step-mother of Chantel's fairy stories. She had instituted sweeping changes, ridding herself of much fine old furniture, replacing it with ornate, uncomfortable pieces.

Only once had Chantel protested. Lydia announced a few weeks after the funeral that her second cousin once removed had taken a position in the city and she had asked him to live with them. "He can have Charles's old room," she added.

"Never!" Chantel sprang to her feet, feeling her face go red and angry tears crowd her eyelids.

11

Lydia's face turned an unbecoming beet color. "We'll see about that!" She stamped out, muttering something about seeing the family solicitor, and returned hours later. Chantel never did discover what the lawyer said, but Lydia scornfully told her, "If you're so upset over it, take Charles's room yourself. Arthur can move into yours."

Lips set, Chantel did as she was told, removing every scrap to show she had occupied the same room since she was born, fiercely resenting the intrusion of a stranger into her home. Yet as slight, dark-haired Arthur Masters unobtrusively did small things for her in a kind, considerate way, her dislike subsided. She even grew grateful for his presence, which seemed to buffer Lydia's and Anita's sarcastic attacks on her.

A loud rumble snapped her to attention. One raindrop hit her hand as she scrambled to her feet. Fear of what would happen should she be discovered or ruin the dress chased at her heels, but she managed to get home, up the stairs, and into her room unseen. Panting, she leaned against her closed door, facing the disheveled image in the great mirror across the room. Who was that tall girl watching her from its depths? Where was the radiant happiness she had thought would be hers when she chose a life companion?

Dismay filled her as she unfastened the gown, breathing a sigh of relief that it was unharmed. She slipped into a simple blue cotton gown and hid the lovely wedding dress out of sight in her closet. Yet she could not shut her thoughts of her fiancé, Arthur Masters. How would he feel, knowing she sat huddled in her room watching the growing storm and wondering if she had been mistaken in accepting his proposal of marriage? Were her doubts only part of what Anita scornfully termed "bridal flutterings"?

She reached for her well-worn Bible, treasured because her father had given it to her. Leafing aimlessly, she read verses here and there, at last reading, "Let not your heart be troubled: ye believe in God, believe also in me." A certain uneasy peace settled over her. Surely God didn't want her to go on and on living in a house where she was disliked. Arthur would provide a home for her, away from Lydia and Anita. Gratitude coursed through her veins. He had been so kind, so understanding, never forcing caresses on her when she involuntarily shrank back. When they were married and away from the ever-present Lydia and Anita, she would welcome his gentle love.

If only he knew her Lord! A frown marred her white forehead. The next moment it smoothed out. He couldn't help but accept the Savior, now that they'd talked about how much He meant to Chantel. There had been humility in his face when he said, "I never had a chance to hear all this before. Give me a little time."

The storm outside had increased. Gigantic cloud armies battled against other equally strong armies, but exhaustion and a measure of hope blotted them out, and Chantel slept.

The flicker of a candle and a "Well! Sleep through dinner while your fiancé waits," bit into her consciousness. Chantel opened drowsy eyes. Her stepsister Anita stood framed in the doorway, candlestick in hand. The next moment she stepped inside, deliberately placed the light where it would shine full on Chantel's face, and sneered, "The little bride-to-be is all tired out, isn't she?"

Chantel had learned not to respond to Anita's taunts. She blinked against the light and lifted one hand to straighten her disorderly hair, so in contrast with Anita's elaborate toilette. The Bible in her lap slid, and she automatically caught it. "Did you want something?" She vaguely heard the rumble of thunder, then sat up straight at Anita's reply.

"Yes. I want you to break your engagement to Arthur."

"Why?" She struggled for words.

"He's never loved you. It's always been me." The glitter in Anita's blue eyes fascinated and held Chantel as the green-gowned girl stepped closer. "Do you think any man would look at you with me around?"

Chantel could feel the blood drain from her face and throat. "I don't believe you."

"Don't you?" The mocking light in her eyes grew stronger. "Ask him. I dare you to ask him and watch his eyes when he answers."

Chantel's mind whirled. In spite of the malice, there was enough truthfulness in Anita's voice to turn the world upside down. She groped for words. "If it's true, then why did he ask me to marry him?"

"For money." Anita stood at Chantel's side now, staring down as she hurled the pitiless words.

"Money!" A great wave of shock swept through Chantel.

"That's right. When you're twenty-one next October, you'll be getting the money your grandmother left." She bared her teeth in a snarl. "Your pious father said we were to be treated as equals, that I'd be given the same as you."

"But you were!" Chantel extricated herself from the chair and faced Anita. In spite of her own height, Anita towered over her. "The will left all Father owned equally divided between you, your mother, and me."

"Paltry sums." Anita's blue eyes were almost black with emotion. "He knew you'd receive ten times as much from your grandmother's legacy."

"He couldn't do anything about that. It was left direct," Chantel defended, hating the scene.

The hard voice tossed more sharp stones. "He could have arranged it. Everyone knows there are ways to get around such things." Bitterness dripped from every word. "He lied."

"Stop!" Chantel seized Anita's arms. "You shall not say those terrible things about Father. He was honorable and good. He would no more think of going against my grandmother's wishes than —" She couldn't get anything else from her blocked-off throat.

16

Anita wrenched free and sent a stinging slap across Chantel's blanched face. "I've always hated you, now most of all." Were the tears in her eyes real or for effect? "Arthur Masters was in love with me. He found out you were to inherit. So he agreed with Mother that —" She clapped her hand to her mouth and turned paler than the snowy counterpane on Chantel's bed.

Chantel reeled, as much from the verbal blow as the impact of the slap. "What do you mean?" she whispered.

"I've said enough." Anita became sullen. "But I'm not going to stand by and let you marry Arthur, have to live here in the same house and see him every day." She laughed wildly. "I won't do it!"

In the charged silence another rumble of the storm shook the house. Then Chantel grabbed her rapidly fleeing senses and demanded, "Why did you say that about living here? We are getting a little cottage across town." She repeated, "Why did you say it?"

"Do you honestly think my mother will allow you and all your money to get away from her?"

Chantel pulled back, appalled at the naked hatred in Anita's face. "It's Arthur who is marrying me. Lydia has no part in it."

The rasp of Anita's half-sobbed words was as grating as the rusty gate had been earlier, sawing into Chantel's nerves. "Arthur is weak. He will do as he's told." Her hatred crumbled into — was it pleading? "You don't love him. Why, you don't even want him to kiss you!" She was rewarded by the hot flush of color in Chantel's face. It served to bring back her usual haughtiness. "What do you think it's going to be like when you are his wife, and he has the right to take what he wants, whether you like it or not?"

Chantel stood rooted to the spot, unable to answer, shame for the terrible things being said changing her from red to white.

Anita cried out, "If you marry him, it will be knowing the lips that kiss you were mine first."

"I don't believe you." Her inane repetition was barely audible while what had once been her heart slowly turned to lead.

"Don't you? Then let me tell you the way he's held me and kissed me and told me that if there were any other way, he'd sell his soul to have me as his wife." Torture lined the shadowed face.

Chantel childishly pressed both hands

over her ears. "I won't listen." Yet deep inside she knew she could never shut out the awful truth.

"You shall listen." Two strong hands took Chantel's own, gripping them until they ached. "He's mine. Do you hear me? Mine!" Anita's eyes dropped to the Bible. "If you're what you say, if you are the great Christian who can do no wrong, you'll never marry a man who by all rights belongs to me."

For the space of a heartbeat, black eyes locked with blue.

"Girls, where are you?" A dapper, smiling man appeared in the open doorway.

Anita's eyes never left Chantel's face. "You can ask him for yourself."

"Ask me what?" Arthur brushed up the ends of his mustache in the mannerism Chantel knew so well.

"Go on. Ask him," Anita ordered, hands still clenching Chantel's.

A voice strangely like her own, but one that couldn't be coming from her throat, startled Chantel. "Anita says you don't love me."

Arthur's mouth widened in a toothy smile, but his dark eyes grew wary. "Dear me. Why would she say such a thing?"

Chantel heard Anita's gasp as she

stepped back. It gave her strength to say, "She told me you'd held her and kissed her and wanted to marry her." The parroted words came in a torrent. "She said you were marrying me for money."

She wasn't prepared for Arthur's reaction. As his eyes narrowed, he cast a disparaging glance toward Anita, then reassured, "She's a jealous fool. She's thrown herself at me ever since I moved in here. It's all I could do to keep away from her."

His bald statement hung in the room. Anita swayed, and in spite of her own misery, Chantel felt a moment of pity.

"She knows I have never loved anyone except you, Chantel."

Was he lying? Anita had said she should watch his eyes. She pulled back her hands from his reaching ones and quietly asked, "Did you and Lydia plan to have us live here after we were married?"

His eyes opened wider, and Chantel moved so he had to face the light to reply. "We did mention it, but of course I said it would be up to you."

"He's lying!" Anita shrilled, appealing to Lydia, who had swept into the room and transfixed them with a stare. "Mother, tell Chantel he doesn't care!"

Lydia's face turned mottled. "Shut up, you little fool!"

Chantel caught the glance between Lydia and Arthur as Anita sobbed and ran from the room. It confirmed the suspicion Anita had planted.

Everything Anita had said was true.

Despair such as she had only known at her father's death threatened to push Chantel into a heap on the floor. From somewhere an unspoken prayer winged its way toward her heavenly Father. *Let me live through these moments, and not break down in front of them.* She opened her mouth, wondering if she could speak. "I'd like to be alone now."

"Chantel," Arthur began.

"Not now." There was something magnificent about her as she stood facing the two who had suddenly become her enemies. Her cry for strength was being answered. Her personal Savior and friend had heard. She knew by heart the verse that came to her mind: "No weapon that is formed against thee shall prosper; and every tongue that shall rise against thee in judgment thou shalt condemn."

"Don't be ridiculous," Lydia snapped, her unhealthy color deepening.

Chantel advanced. "We will discuss it

later." She had unconsciously chosen the same words she had heard her father use to end uncomfortable arguments. Even Lydia retreated from them. She and Arthur stepped into the hall and Chantel closed the door behind them, locking it securely. A little later she heard angry voices down the hall, perhaps from Anita's room. Were Arthur and Lydia scourging the younger girl for telling the truth?

Hours later Chantel still sat huddled in the chair, heedless of the storm that had battered Boston before being blown away by a fresh, healing breeze. The candle guttered and went out. It didn't matter; dawn was near. She had spent the night in soul-searching and prayer. Strangely enough, there was no sense of loss, only a deep, wonderful gladness that she had found out in time what Arthur Masters was. She had weighed Anita's accusations about not loving Arthur and found them true. Thinking of Anita in Arthur's arms repelled her. Was that why he had been willing to forego affection from Chantel? He was no longer the defender, but the hunter, in Chantel's new awareness.

Facing the truth had been her Gethsemane. She was as much to blame as Arthur. She knew the Lord Jesus Christ. She knew her life could never be fulfilled and happy with a nonbeliever. How she had grasped at straws to convince herself that Arthur was that chosen companion, how gullible she had been, how eager to believe he would confess himself a sinner and accept her Lord!

Excusing herself because she'd never really been attracted to a man before didn't help. Little talks with her father before he died should have prepared her.

"God," she cried out at one point, "how can anyone ever be willing to trust herself to a man's care?" Memory of Anita's wild, almost mindless love haunted her. Better to live alone all her days than become like that.

In the early morning she knelt by the open window. She was spent, uncertain as to what would happen next, yet a sense of escape filled her troubled heart. She could not totally free herself from Anita's words, shuddering at their implication. What she had felt for Arthur was gratitude mingled with the desire to be cared for. It wasn't enough. It never could be.

"I've run ahead of You, God, looking for a deliverer when all the time I've had Your Son." Remorse mingled with shame. "Forgive me for not trusting You."

A few reaching fingers of rosy color touched the silver sky. Somewhere a bird called to his mate. The sound of horses and carriages pierced Chantel's consciousness. She raised her head. A beautiful June day was dawning. A newly washed, cleansed world awaited her and her freshly awakened determination to follow her Lord.

But far on the horizon, over the tops of houses, another bank of storm clouds lurked, as if waiting their best opportunity to attack.

2

Chantel held up the filmy skirts of her dainty morning gown as she descended the stairs. In spite of the assurance that had come from her night's tryst, her heart beat wildly when Lydia confronted her at the bottom of the stairway.

Her stepmother must not have slept, either. Her face was ravaged, whether from loss of sleep or anger, Chantel could not tell. Her usually perfectly arranged hair was carelessly piled on top of her head, and her ice-blue eyes glittered, much as Anita's had done the night before. "Come into the library."

Chantel shivered a bit but obeyed, sending another quick prayer upward.

Lydia slowly closed the massive carved door and leaned against it. Her eyes were accusing. "Now, what's all this nonsense about? I could get nothing out of Anita except that you two had had a cat-and-parrot fight."

Chantel stifled the desire to giggle. The description was so perfect for the candlelit scene the night before. To give herself time, she let her gaze sweep the library. Outside of her own room, it was the only room in the house left as her father had furnished it. Rich bindings on good books she and her father had read together brought back memories. She blinked hard.

Lydia was only getting wound up. "First of all, what insane idea possessed you to go running to the cemetery in your wedding dress?" Horror filled her voice, and she raised her hands in an almost threatening gesture. "Don't you have any sense at all?"

"How did you know?" Chantel's question was also an admission.

"I have eyes in my head, don't I?" The cold expression grew even chillier. "Well, why did you do it?"

Chantel felt the same way she had felt as a small child called before her stepmother for some infraction. "I — I wanted to be close to Father." She faltered. "The dressmaker had just finished the gown, and I thought —"

"Saints preserve us from such as you." Lydia's rage knew no bounds. "Your father is dead. Can't you get that through your head? Running to a cemetery in a wedding gown! I ought to have you put away for the public good." Some of the anger dwindled, as if a new and pleasant idea had crossed Lydia's mind.

"It doesn't matter. I won't be using the dress."

"You have another guess coming, young lady. If you think I'll let you turn down Arthur Masters because of some little quarrel, you are wrong. The wedding will go on as planned, two weeks from today."

For one ghastly moment Chantel wondered if Lydia could force her to marry Arthur. She grasped at the slipping reins of freedom. "Arthur and Anita are in love."

"You're as much of a fool as they are." Fury contorted Lydia's features. "Do you think any man doesn't amuse himself with a pretty girl when he can?" Her laugh was brittle, as if a delicate glass had been shattered into fragments against the brick fireplace.

"My father wouldn't," Chantel asserted.

Grudging admiration warred with Lydia's sophistication. "No. But he was hopelessly old-fashioned. Nowadays a flirtation means nothing. Once you're settled down here married, Arthur won't care a straw for Anita. She won't even be here. I'm planning on enrolling her in a good girls' school."

"You honestly think I will agree to marrying Arthur now?" Her incredulous expression was like oil on a hot fire.

"Of course! I've explained that it doesn't mean a thing." Lydia threw wide the library door, motioning in the man standing on the threshold. "Come in, Arthur. I believe we've about closed our discussion."

There wasn't a hint about the well-turned-out man that there had ever been a rift. "Good morning, my dear. How lovely you look!"

Chantel drew back from his outstretched hands. To think she had ever thought she could be this man's wife! Loathing for him mingled with self-disgust. No wonder the Lord had had to teach her a lesson. Thank God it had come before she was legally bound.

"There seemed to be some question about the wedding." Lydia bridged the gap of silence.

Her words triggered Chantel's response. Back against the fireplace, she stated, "There will be no wedding."

Arthur merely smiled at Lydia. "If you will excuse us, I believe I can get this all straightened out." He waited until Lydia reluctantly left the room then smiled and advanced. "Chantel, you mustn't believe what Anita said. She's never meant anything to me."

She could see the flicker deep in his eyes that betrayed him. It wouldn't have mattered anyway, not after her all-night vigil and soul-searching. "Don't touch me, Arthur." Her quiet voice halted him, although the smile still lingered. "I have made a mistake. I can't marry you. Ever." She caught his movement and held up one hand. "It isn't just because of Anita. I've discovered I don't love you the way a woman should love a man she marries."

Quicker than a cat after a mouse, Arthur had her pinioned in his arms. She hadn't dreamed he was so strong. His lips stopped hers in a long kiss. She couldn't even struggle. He held her too tightly. When he released her, he stepped back and laughed triumphantly. "Now, can you still say you don't love me? I should have done that weeks ago." He brushed up his mustache the way he had the night before and added, "I can hardly wait until we're married. I'll teach you what love is — and you'll like it."

Chantel scrubbed her lips furiously to get rid of the hated kisses. "I despise you more than anyone on earth!" She took advantage of his open-mouthed shock and flung open the library door, nearly upset-

29

ting the eavesdropping Lydia.

"Chantel, wait!"

But she was gone, faster than a speeding carriage, straight to the refuge of the room that had been her father's. All the pounding on the door that followed brought no response from the white-faced girl who sobbed soundlessly into her pillow.

At last they went away. The house was quiet. It was only after Chantel heard the carriage and saw them drive away that she dared venture down the back way and to the cemetery. She could always hide in the shrubbery if they followed her there.

What was she to do? They couldn't make her marry Arthur. She could close her mouth and refuse to speak. Yet she must have help. "God, for Jesus' sake, show me what to do."

A long time later she stood, aware of how weak she was. No wonder — she had gone without dinner or breakfast or lunch. She must eat. She cautiously crept back to the house and into the kitchen, finding bread and cheese and a glass of milk. She didn't want to see anyone else that night. She didn't even make a light to undress by. Let them think she had gone to bed early. She needed the time to plan.

She must go away. She could not stay in

this house any longer. Even though her heart cried out in protest, she set her lips firmly and stared unseeing into the soft night. Where could she go? What should she do? For the first time she regretted the love of her father, who had encouraged her in books and music, laughingly telling her there would always be enough money to provide for her. While other girls had learned to make their way in the world, she had idly dreamed away her days in a round of pleasantness.

Chantel mentally ran through the list of occupations girls less fortunate than she used to make their way: nurse, teacher, cook. She sighed. She had no training for any of them!

"I wonder if the law would let me draw some of my grandmother's inheritance? How much is there from Father?" she speculated. "I should have asked about such things, instead of leaving it to Lydia." The great world suddenly became frightening. "Why haven't I had a talk with Mr. Barker?" The June night, with its scent of roses in the air, had no answers. "I'll go tomorrow," she resolved. With a prayer on her lips, she fell asleep.

"Why, Miss Evans!" There was no mistaking the pleasure on Mr. Barker's face the next morning. Chantel had arisen early and was waiting in his office when he arrived.

"Come in, come in." He hung his hat on a stand and cordially ushered her into his private rooms. "What can I do for you?"

His kindly manner, coupled with the familiar round face and keen eyes behind his spectacles, nearly undid Chantel's vow not to blurt out the truth. She had decided to discover what she could without making accusations about Lydia. Any scandal would only reflect on her beloved father's memory.

"I was wondering if I could get some extra money before it's time for my quarterly allowance."

"Of course." He stepped to the door and called to his secretary, "Bring me the Evans folder, please."

Chantel held her breath as he opened it and frowned. On the way to the office this morning, she'd decided the best thing to do was get enough money to find a quiet room, perhaps in some respectable lady's home, and wait until October fifth, when her grandmother's legacy would come to her.

"Is anything the matter?" she asked when

Mr. Barker didn't immediately speak.

"It's just that the balance has dwindled drastically in the past few months." He bent his keen gaze on her. "Miss Evans, that must be quite a trousseau you're gathering. See here." He showed her a row of withdrawals. "There are only a few hundred dollars left. I hadn't realized . . ." Doubt crept into his voice. "How could you have used so much?" A wave of red stained his face, and he held up one hand before Chantel could reply. "Sorry. It isn't really any of my business. I was just shocked for a moment."

"May I take a closer look?" Chantel bent over the figures. She focused on them, noting the withdrawal days. "Why, I haven't —" She clamped her teeth into her lower lip and halted any more words.

"Mrs. Evans has been picking up the money for you." Mr. Barker pointed. "Here, and here, and here. All I can say is, it is going to be some wedding, if this is any indication!" Disapproval shone for a moment and was replaced by a business-like manner. "Now, how much do you want?"

Chantel forced her gloved fingers to lie still in her lap. Nausea threatened her. She must not tell Mr. Barker she had received only a few dollars of all that had been withdrawn. She remembered vaguely signing a permission slip for Lydia to pick up money from her account after the funeral, when she was too dazed to care. Lydia must have used it again and again.

"What I was really wondering is if there's any way I could draw on my grandmother's legacy."

Every trace of friendliness vanished. "I'm sorry, Miss Evans. That is impossible. It clearly reads that the money is to be paid to you on your twenty-first birthday." He cleared his throat. "By the way, there may be a hold on that payment." He bent an ivory letter opener back and forth while Chantel's nerves screamed. "I received word this morning that your stepmother had registered a protest in her daughter's name concerning the inheritance."

So that's where Lydia and Arthur went yesterday. Aloud, Chantel said, "Is that possible? My father said it was all clearly stated."

The letter opener snapped. Mr. Barker flung the two pieces onto his desk. "I haven't had the opportunity to recheck the exact wording."

Chantel's world blackened. Through the thick cloud she heard herself ask, "Then I

34

may not get the inheritance?"

"It will depend on the way it is written. If your grandmother stated you specifically, there's no problem. If it was written that it was to be jointly shared by your father's heirs, then Anita will probably be granted a share. In any event, it may drag on for a time. A wily attorney can produce all kinds of evidence."

"I see." Chantel marveled that she could stand without swaying. A dozen ideas raced through her head and were as rapidly rejected. One thing stood out: She must get what money there was left away from here before Lydia closed it out and she was left penniless. "I'd like to withdraw the rest of my father's legacy, please, if that's all right."

Disapproval again gleamed in the usually genial face. "I dislike seeing you do that, Miss Evans, but your father left instructions that you might do so if you ever chose." He ushered her into the other room. "If you will wait a few minutes, I will have a check prepared."

"Could I have it in cash instead, please?"

"Certainly." The word dripped icicles. He disappeared into another room, and presently his secretary called to Chantel, "Here is your money." She counted it out while Chantel cringed, face flaming. The secretary's countenance was as disapproving as Mr. Barker's had been. Chantel wished she could cry out in her own defense, but loyalty to her father's memory kept her silent.

She stumbled down the steps to the street, reticule clutched tightly under her cloak. All she had in the world to depend on was in the small pouch. She must not lose it. Yet as she passed a red brick church with its white spire pointing to heaven she was comforted. Someone was with her, and His loving care was more to be treasured than earthly possessions.

Waving away a carriage that pulled alongside, Chantel walked the long way home. Never had Boston been lovelier. Flowers were everywhere. The skies smiled and birds sang. People she met seemed affected by the rare day and beamed at her. She managed a tremulous smile in return, temporarily putting her problems away, but when she arrived home, they met her full force.

"And where have you been?" Lydia demanded from the doorway.

"I went on an errand."

It passed. Anita was nowhere in sight, but Arthur lounged in the hall doorway. "I have something to say to you." Lydia gestured toward the library.

For a single moment Chantel rebelled. After the harrowing findings at Mr. Barker's office, she couldn't face Lydia. Still, if she didn't face her now, it would have to be done later. She might as well get it over with.

"Arthur tells me you are stubbornly persisting in your own way."

Chantel cast a defiant glance at Arthur before she replied. "I believe I can best choose my life."

"You're nothing but a baby who needs a keeper. You've been petted and spoiled ever since I've known you. Well, you can just get this through your head: I am not going to stand for it. The wedding will take place as planned." Lydia warmed to her subject. "Even if I allowed you your own way in this, what would you do? You can't think Anita and I want you sniveling around here."

"I can find a position."

"You?" All Chantel's inner shortcomings flared in the indictment. "What are you good for?"

"I can be a governess." Chantel held her ground.

"So, you would shame your father's

memory by becoming a common servant! I'd see you put away first." Lydia dabbed at her eyes with a scrap of handkerchief.

"Why are you so anxious for me to marry Arthur?" Chantel determined to know the truth, to see if Anita had been right. "If you're trying to get rid of me, this isn't the way. Why should you care anything about what I do?"

The widow sanctimoniously folded her hands. "Your father left you as my responsibility, whether I like it or not. I intend to see you are taken care of."

It was all Chantel could do not to shout with laughter. The idea of Lydia caring about her was preposterous. She hadn't even cared for her as a child, let alone after she grew up. But what point was there in arguing? "I'm sorry, Lydia." She turned toward the door. "I just can't marry Arthur."

"You can and you will." The ultimatum followed Chantel up the staircase.

Three uneasy days crept by, then one afternoon Lydia burst into the house, absolutely livid. "Chantel, how dare you humiliate me?" She towered over the white-clad figure reading in a corner of the library.

Chantel raised astonished eyes. "What did I do?"

"Don't act so pure and innocent, you deceitful thing. I went to Mr. Barker's office to get money to pay for the caterer. I've never been so mortified in my entire life. He told me you'd been in and withdrawn everything left in the account your father left!"

"It was mine." Chantel turned away from the hateful stare of her stepmother. "You've been taking the money, and all I got was the few dollars I asked for to get a few things."

"You wicked, ungrateful child! Do you think a wedding is free?" Her blond hair threatened to free itself from its moorings and fall wild. "It costs money to make dresses and hire a hall and musicians."

"It's hard to believe it cost all those hundreds of dollars." Chantel rose. She could defend herself better on her feet. She had prayed for patience, but this must be settled. "I've told you I am not getting married. Besides," she took a quick breath. "Lydia, a lot of the money was withdrawn before Arthur ever came here."

"Are you calling me a thief?" Something akin to fear blended with Lydia's icy anger. "Are you forgetting the mourning clothing and expenses for your father's funeral? I of course assumed you wished to be responsible for those."

"Please, Lydia, let's not argue." Chantel's colorless face set. "Forget the past. Just let me alone. As soon as I can, I'll leave here and you will be rid of me."

"If you dare leave this house without my permission, I'll order the police to drag you back." The deadly threat was more effective than Lydia's anger had ever been. "If I have to, I'll prove you aren't responsible for your actions."

Chantel stood speechless.

"Oh, yes, I can prove it." Lydia stepped closer. "Girls don't moon over graves. Or visit them in wedding gowns. Or deliberately withdraw money and plan to run away from home. Not unless they're deranged." She hesitated to see the full impact of her statement. "Or unless they are — bad."

Scarlet strands rushed into Chantel's face. For an instant she longed to throw her purse into the accusing, gloating face. Instead she turned and walked quietly out the door, leaving Arthur and Lydia alone. In her room she hastily searched out a little cloth bag, stuffed the bills Mr. Barker had given her into it, and pinned the bag securely inside her dress. In order to obtain the money, Lydia would have to search her.

"I have to get away, God. But how? Where?"

For hours she wrestled with the problem. If only she had relatives or friends who would open their homes! Her father had been so all-satisfying that she'd never cared about having friends her own age. He had even preferred to educate her himself, so she had been denied schoolmates. The only living relative she had was Grandfather Evans, and he lived in the wilds of western Montana Territory on a cattle ranch. He might as well be in Europe for all the help he'd be.

From stories her father told, Charles Evans, Sr., was a crusty, self-willed man. When his only son longed for more than life on the ranch, there had been a terrible argument and Chantel's father had traveled east to settle in Boston. The years had passed without reconciliation. After Charles, Jr., became a Christian he had written to his father but received no answer. The only sign they had that he was still alive was an annual gift to Chantel, who had been named for her grandmother and the little town Charles, Sr., founded in southwestern Montana Territory.

For a second she played with the idea of appealing to him for help but immediately rejected it. Surely such a desperate measure would not be needed! She sprang up to pace the floor. In the last three days she had made a few fumbling overtures about finding a job as a governess. Every interview had gone the same: surprised and pleased reactions to her knowledge of books and music, followed by scowls for her lack of references. No one was willing to take an unknown into her home. She couldn't blame them. Neither would she use her full name, but had applied as simply Miss Evans.

Now the days raced by. Each left Chantel more discouraged, her faith wearing thin. God must deliver her. She had made no further protest about the wedding plans. If Lydia chose to go ahead, let her. It at least kept her from haunting Chantel. When the wedding was barely a week away, Lydia came in with spots of red in her cheeks. She had been almost affable since Chantel had been keeping silent.

"We're all invited to *the* Carter Vanderveers'" this weekend," she announced, preening before a gilt-edged mirror. Her hair had been freshly done and shimmered in the sunlight streaming into the hall.

Between fear, depression, and a raging headache, Chantel's dark eyes were dull.

"Go without me, please." She knew better than to refuse outright. "I don't feel well at all."

Lydia glanced at her, noticing the dark circles under her eyes. "Heavens, what a washed-out bride you're going to be!" She turned to Arthur. "Should we let her stay behind and rest?"

"Whatever she chooses. After all, one week from now she'll be with me all the time."

Chantel hid her anger at his possessive tone and meekly said, "I really do want you all to go." Her eyes rested on Anita, whose gratitude showed. As they went out to get ready, Anita lingered, a curious moistness in her blue eyes. "Thank you, Chantel." She started to say more but was stopped by her mother's impatient call from the stairs, telling her to hurry, the carriage would soon call for them.

Chantel breathed a sigh of relief when they had gone. Then she dropped to a chair, hands pressed to her pounding temples. "God, is this Your way of giving me a chance to escape?" She relaxed her tense muscles. "I still don't know where to go." Memories of long walks and talks with her father spun before her tired eyes, and a scene she had nearly forgotten replayed itself. She hadn't been more than ten. In a burst of love for her father, she'd thrown herself into his lap and said, "I love you best of anything in the whole world."

His arms had closed around her. "And you are precious." She could still feel the comfort of those strong encircling arms.

Longing to again be comforted, she slowly unlocked a trunk where some of his things had been put. One by one she touched the treasures: a stone they'd picked up on a walk, little gifts from Grandfather Evans. Strange, how he couldn't forgive his son but took time from his busy life to send her remembrances!

Her searching fingers delved deeper. In the very bottom of the trunk was a picture. Why, it could have been her father! Yet the blurred inscription on it read, "Charles Evans, 1829." It must be her grandfather shortly before her father had been born.

She peered at the image. The likeness was uncanny, as if a younger edition of her father looked back at her. The same steady eyes, the same strong arms. Chantel felt a pulse of excitement. A few days ago she had considered appealing to Grandfather Evans as a last desperate measure. Now she was down to just that. She had tried for work, to no avail; she had tried to reason with Lydia, with even poorer results.

Had God led her to search the old trunk when she most needed guidance? It seemed an odd way for Him to answer, but then, why should she feel any of His ways were odd?

Chantel started to replace the daguerreotype, hesitated, then searched the features once more. A little warmth grew within her. She clutched the picture and closed the trunk, wondering if she dared follow the leadings of her heart and the look in her grandfather's eyes that seemed to offer an invitation.

3

Chantel slowly made her way through the doors of the railroad station. Several men looked at her curiously, and she drew back from their bold stares. She could feel the blood pounding in her temples as she waited until a ticket agent was free.

"Help you, miss?" The bearded agent looked at her curiously.

She tried twice before her voice would come. "Can you tell me how much it costs to go to Montana Territory?"

"Montana Territory!" He whistled through his teeth. "A pretty little gal like you going way out there?" He scratched his balding head. "Something wrong with our Boston boys?"

A guffaw from the onlookers spurred Chantel's dignity. "My grandfather lives there."

Her cool reply dampened the agent's enthusiasm for jokes. "Where in Montana Territory?"

"A little place called Chantel." She held her breath as he ran a grimy finger down a listing and regretfully shook his head. "Sorry. No train to any place like that. Just where is it?"

She closed her eyes hard, concentrating, trying to remember conversations with her father. "It's between the Rocky Mountains and the Bitterroots, in southwestern Montana." She scanned the worn map he shoved in front of her, searching for a familiar name. "Oh, I remember. It's about a hundred miles southwest of Butte." She pointed a gloved finger at a little dot.

The dour face split in a grin. "Well, I'll say you're in luck! Up until last year, you could only have gone to Ogden and then hired someone to take you into Montana Territory. Just last December they went and opened a spur line." He traced the wavy marks on the map, and Chantel's fascinated eyes followed. "Called it the Utah and Northern." His head almost touched Chantel's as they bent over the map. "According to what you tell me, this Chantel's got to be maybe twenty-some miles west of Dillon." He moved his finger to a smaller dot. "They up and named the principal town on the line Dillon, after the president of the Utah and Northern, Sidney Dillon.

You can change from the Union Pacific at Ogden and ride the new line practically to where you want to get."

"I think maybe God had the new railroad be there when I needed it."

The agent scratched his head. "Think so? I thought it was the Utah and Northern that did the job. But then I've been mistook before."

Chantel's face flamed. Why had she let her gratitude spill over? Suddenly the room seemed uncomfortably warm, as if the loungers' eyes were boring into her back. She had called attention to herself when what she should have done was just inquire.

Fumbling with her reticule, she slowly withdrew the amount the agent asked for and tucked her ticket away. She managed to thank him and walk the gauntlet of eyes to the door.

"Train leaves early Tuesday, miss." The station agent had turned cooperative. "Don't be late."

"I won't." She paused and smiled, seeing admiration creep into his face, but all the way home she was amazed at her daring. She had dipped into her little hoard and bought a ticket to Montana Territory and a grandfather she had never seen!

One by one she faced her knotty problems as she slowly walked, little heeding the June day that would have been an invitation to her earlier. "Thank You," she whispered, taking care that no one else heard her. Lydia's threat to have her put away was still very real. Yet the same feeling of being cared for that had sprung up on seeing her grandfather's picture and finding the railroad went to Dillon warmed her frightened heart.

There was so much to be done! How could she accomplish it all and be gone before Lydia, Arthur, and Anita returned Sunday night? Could she act normally all day Monday? They must not suspect her! Her errant feet led her to a bench in a small park nearby. Screened by trees, she bowed her head. "Dear Father, You've helped me this far. Please, for Jesus' sake, help me do what I have to do." Her lips quivered. "Amen."

She felt better, as if the load she carried had been cut in two and someone had taken the heavier part. She stood, walked rapidly, and planned as she went.

First, the servants. Would they be a help or hindrance? Father had hired both cook and maid, but Lydia chose her own gardener after old Sam died. She considered confiding in Becky the cook and decided against it with a definite shake of her head. Becky and Annie had been keeping out of sight as much as possible the past weeks. Surely they knew what was going on, but they couldn't really help. She sighed. Somehow she would have to get them out of the house.

Next came her clothing, her father's small treasures, and the books. If they were left behind, Lydia would sell or give them away. She would have to pack and arrange for them to be shipped.

A qualm interrupted her planning. Here she was planning to ship her earthly possessions across country to an unknown place! Her chin firmed. If Grandfather Evans didn't want her, she'd find some kind of work, maybe in Butte. She'd scrub floors before she would return to Boston, at least until after the matter of her grandmother's inheritance was settled. As soon as she was twenty-one, she'd write Mr. Barker and tell him where she was.

Could she ever do it all? There was no choice. She must.

Her first battle was with the servants. It proved surprisingly easy. She had no more than gone inside when a weeping Annie accosted her, her hardworking red hands clasped together. "Miss Chantel, my father's been took real sick. They sent my brother to tell me. What can I do?"

Chantel's heart leaped. "Why, you must go to him, of course!"

"But how can I leave you here alone? With all the family gone? Mrs. Evans came back a bit ago, said she forgot something. Didn't stay long enough for me to tell her."

"It's all right, Annie." Chantel smiled into the troubled eyes and took the rough hand. "You go on home. I'll be praying for your father," she added shyly.

"Oh, miss, God bless you!"

The fervent thanks rang in Chantel's ears as she helped Annie get ready and put her in a carriage, paying the driver from her own precious store of money. Relief danced through her. Now for Becky. She stepped into the kitchen. The purring calico cat and sunny room quieted her racing spirit.

"What time you want dinner, dear?" The black face with its wide smile welcomed her.

Chantel glanced at the ticking clock on the window ledge. "Not for awhile." She made up her mind to plunge boldly into what must be done. "Becky, I want you to help me pack some things."

"Like Master Charles's things?" A flash of understanding crossed between them.

"Yes." Chantel choked but forced back the rush of emotion the good old woman's insight had stirred. "His books don't mean much to Mrs. Evans. I also want you to go see that son of yours and his children this weekend."

"Leave you here alone?" Becky threw her apron up in horror. "I just saw Annie leaving because her pa's sick." The great oxlike eyes rolled. "Who's going to see you eat right?"

Chantel braced herself. "I have to learn to do things for myself, Becky."

Becky reluctantly gave a little ground. "With your getting married, I s'pose you do."

Chantel seized on it. "Any girl old enough to get married is old enough to take care of herself for a few days."

Becky heaved herself up and waddled toward the pantry. "At least there's plenty of vittles. Won't take much doing."

"I'll be fine, Becky." On impulse, Chantel gave the old woman a big hug. Parting with her would be painful, but even more so if Becky ever suspected what Chantel was about to do. She'd taken care of Chantel since Chantel's mother died, as best she could with Lydia always present, using her wages to help her son and his family.

"Let me get into an old gown and we'll start. Not that any books in this house could be dusty! You and Annie see to that."

The dark face glowed with pride. "Annie's a good girl and hardworking. Some fella will be carrying her off, I expect." Becky's hands were already busy with boxes from the storeroom. "You run along and get out of that good dress."

Chantel's heart was lighter than it had been in days as she ran upstairs and down the hall. Why was her bedroom door open? She was sure she'd closed it before leaving.

She stepped inside and gasped. Her peaceful room looked as if a hurricane had gone through it. Bureau drawers were open, contents mussed. The white counterpane was half off the bed, the pillows awry. The wardrobe door stood open, revealing clothing shoved together and shoes out of place. The room had been ransacked.

"Lydia!" Annie had said Lydia had come back. The truth hit Chantel with stunning force: Lydia had been looking for the money hidden safely in Chantel's dress with her ticket to freedom.

She sank weakly to a chair, still unbelieving. "I didn't think she would go so far." Yet memory of her stepmother's threats should have warned her.

"Why you so slow, honey?" Becky's voice preceded her ponderous footsteps.

Chantel sprang into action. Even Becky must not know what Lydia had done. "Don't come up. I'll be right down." Her nerveless fingers struggled with her dress and finally got a favorite old cotton fastened. She closed her bedroom door behind her. She'd straighten it out later. Spots of determination colored her face as she went to the library. "All right, Becky, let's start sorting." She could not take everything. She must not leave great spaces for Lydia to notice and question. Scalding tears fell as she weighed values, finally choosing those volumes with the most memories.

Dusk had given way to night when Becky was reluctantly shooed away. "I won't be easy till I get back."

"I'll be fine." Chantel watched the sturdy figure plod down the street and out of her life, then, her lips set in a grim line, she locked the doors on the inside, put chairs under the knobs so not even a key could let someone in unawares, and set to work.

When it was all done, it was a pitifully small heap to represent twenty years: a few mementoes she could not bear to leave behind; serviceable clothing of cotton and wool; a few of her prettiest trousseau frocks she couldn't bear to leave. She would have little use for party frocks. She must take what would last and be proper for life in the wilderness.

By Sunday night she was ready. Her trunk had already gone, carried off by a drayman along with the nailed box of books. Her closet was arranged so the missing clothing was not noticeable. The carpetbag she would carry on the train was ready to hold her toilet articles, to be fitted in with a dressing gown at the last minute. Pictures of her father and little-remembered mother lay smothered in cloth. Her Bible would go on top.

Chantel was so tired that her evening prayers were short but heartfelt. How smoothly everything had gone so far. If — she was too tired to complete the thought.

She had been asleep when she heard the carriage stop in front of the house. A moment of bewildered fear passed. They would not disturb her tonight. She heard Becky's rumbled, "Yessum, Miss Chantel's done gone to bed," then muffled laughter on the stairs. Anita and Arthur? It didn't matter. If she could make it through one more day and night, she would be safe.

Monday did not start auspiciously. Chantel came downstairs to find Lydia scolding Annie. "You actually dared leave this house without my permission?"

Annie cast a frightened glance at Chantel but didn't speak.

"I gave her permission to go," Chantel said.

Lydia's anger diverted to Chantel, and Annie scuttled away. "You! Since when did you become mistress of this house?"

The temptation to shout that she was daughter of the house and that should be enough rose in Chantel, but memory of her quiet time with her Bible and a silvery dawn helped her say, "Annie's father was very ill, I sent her to him." She forced herself to ask, "Did you have a good time at the Vanderveers'?" Not that she cared. It simply was a way to distract Lydia, who loved bragging about her social successes.

It didn't work this time. Lydia merely swept her an angry glance and said, "I'm going to see Mr. Barker this afternoon. It's high time we settled this whole business of what you think you can do." She held out a white, perfectly groomed hand. "I want that money you withdrew from Mr. Barker."

Lydia's effrontery shocked Chantel, although she'd decided nothing could shock her after finding her room searched.

"I know you have it. I need it to pay some bills. Wedding bills." Her eyes never left Chantel's face. "Tiresome people want to be paid even before they perform their services, and I'm certainly not taking Anita's and my inheritance for them."

Chantel's silence seemed to enrage her. "Give me that money! I know you have it. It isn't in your room."

"You wouldn't dare speak to me so if Father hadn't died." Chantel's intention to be still lay in fragments at her feet. "Why are you so anxious to marry me to Arthur? Why insist on a wedding I have told you can never take place?"

"And I have said it shall." Lydia was relentless. "Do you think I'll let all I've waited for slip away because you must have your own way? Never! I married Charles for money, nothing else."

"You managed to hide your reasons, Lydia." Chantel was horrified at her own voice; she was stooping to Lydia's level. Realization turned her pale. In spite of her good intentions, she had come dangerously close to sounding like a shrieking fish-monger.

Lydia didn't even appear disturbed. "I can be clever when I choose. Now, are you going to give me that money, or must I tell Mr. Barker you're unbalanced and need a strong guardian?"

Her full intention dropped into place as Chantel's mind recoiled. No matter which way it went, Lydia planned to win. If Arthur, weak and willing to accept Lydia's direction, married Chantel, control would still be in Lydia's hands. If she refused, they would swear she was incapable of handling her own money, using evidence cleverly to show that Lydia was a concerned stepmother caring for a sacred trust.

Yet in that moment of despair, that same strong feeling of her Savior going ahead of her to smooth the path helped her whisper, "You must do as you will, Lydia. So must I." She turned on trembling legs and stepped out the back door, automatically seeking refuge at her father's grave.

Hours later Lydia summoned Arthur to the library. From her vantage point in her bedroom, Chantel had seen the distress in her stepmother's face. Never in her life had Chantel sneaked around or eavesdropped, yet now she crept down the stairs, out the door, and positioned herself under an open library window, hidden by great lilac bushes that broadcast their fragrance into the night. *"God, I hate this, but I have to know what they are planning next."* A merry breeze lifted her dark hair and cooled her flushed face.

Arthur's voice sent shivers through her. "What did Barker tell you?" His question was harsh.

"That this house belongs to Chantel."

"What?" The word rang like a shot, sending shivers up the listening girl's spine. "You told me it was yours!"

Her stepmother's sullen reply was low but clear. "I thought it was. I never knew the house came to her from her maternal grandmother through her mother. The same grandmother who's leaving her the inheritance."

"Does Chantel have any idea it's hers?"

"Of course not! Do you think she'd stand us for a minute if she did?" Supreme scorn dripped into the night air. "She isn't going to find out, either."

Arthur groaned. "Barker will tell her. You can count on that."

"He can't. He's an old-fashioned man who will carry out the letter of his instructions." A brittle laugh. "For once, I'm glad.

She's to be given the deed to the house along with her inheritance on the day she's twenty-one. Charles was given life occupancy only."

"October fifth is still months away!"

"She's got to marry you. Otherwise we're all out."

From her hiding place Chantel could see Lydia pacing the library floor. What if she should notice the missing books? Yet how insignificant they were, compared to what was happening.

Lydia continued, "The only other way is to prove her unstable. Of course it would mean a lot of gossip, but it could be done. Or perhaps we could get her away to a private institution."

Chantel covered her mouth with her hands to hold back a cry. How evil they were! How maddened for money and power! Never had she encountered sin in such a form. Her sheltered life had protected her from all but Lydia's rages when her father was absent. She inadvertently shifted position, and the lilacs rustled.

"What was that?"

Chantel ducked low at Arthur's question. Sheer terror drove away any sense of security. To be discovered now was to lose every hope of escape.

"Probably a stray animal." Lydia sounded irritated. "Close the window and we'll plan what to do if she still refuses . . ." The scrape of the sash cut off the sentence.

Chantel waited until the library lights were extinguished before creeping from the bushes. Step by cautious step she stole up the back way to her room and heaved a great sigh when she was safely behind the locked door.

But the fight was not over. It had barely begun.

Through the dark hours Chantel waged war against the two forces pulling her.

This was her home, the ancestral home built so many years before. She loved it, despite the unhappiness Lydia and Anita had brought. She had the right to force them to leave, once she was twenty-one.

What if she went to Mr. Barker and told him the whole thing? Would he understand and believe her? Why had he told Lydia the terms of the arrangement? She brushed aside the question. It wasn't important. What was important was the decision she had to make. This night she must decide to either make public the greed and grasping of the woman her father had married or carry out her own plans and leave.

Even if Mr. Barker believed her, the city would gloat as every sordid detail was brought out. Lydia would fight, perhaps accuse her of insanity.

"No." The single syllable burst through her locked lips. She could not smirch her father's memory by having this quarrel brought into the open. It was a commandment of God that father and mother should be honored. There would be no honor in having a daughter tell the world the terrible things going on in her father's home.

Yet was it right to slink away and leave everything to Lydia? Chantel's love for her home, the hundreds of little reminders of happier days, rose to confront her decision.

"Why did you ever marry her?" she asked the picture she dug from the bottom of her carpetbag. There was no answer in the image before her. Perhaps it had been to give her a new mother, someone to care. Lydia had been careful never to criticize Chantel before her father. She had even been friendly at times. Now Chantel knew that all that time it had been for the money, just as Arthur planned to marry her for money.

"God, how far from marriage as You created it to be!" Chantel rocked back and forth, dry-eyed. "At least, I've escaped Arthur." Or had she? Over and over the thought came bringing fear that filled every fiber of her body. Only by gripping her Bible and murmuring inaudible prayers for help could she still herself and clear her mind.

White-faced, spent after hours on her knees, Chantel raised herself wearily as daylight sent exploring rays into her room. She could not stay. She would go. Maybe someday, if everything was settled without bringing dishonor to the Evans name, she could return, but it would never be home again.

Squinting her eyes, she took a small piece of paper and wrote, "I cannot marry Arthur. I am going away."

She pinned it to her pillowcase, picked up her carpetbag and reticule, and holding her shoes in one hand, stole through her door. Her heart was full to bursting, but she never looked back. In the privacy of early dawn she put on her shoes and began her long journey.

4

It felt like a hundred miles to the railway station. Chantel had been tempted to arrange for a carriage but decided against it. There would be an outcry when she was discovered missing. No one, not even a driver, must know when or just how she had left the house.

The carpetbag pulled on her arm, forcing her to rest often, but fear of missing her train goaded her on. Just before she reached her destination, she took a long, dark veil and wound it around her head and face, afraid the agent might remember she had bought a ticket for the journey and call attention to her. She must be obscure, a passenger no different from other passengers in any way. Her dark blue traveling suit was well cut but unobtrusive. Her black hat and shoes had been chosen for the same reason.

She made the station with minutes to

spare, spending them apart from the other sleepy people who would be on the journey with her. Once she heard someone cry, "There she is!" and nearly fainted. When she turned her head it was to see a tall man holding a girl in his arms. Overwhelming gladness that it was not Arthur coming for her turned her knees to water, and she could barely make it across the platform and into the train when it was time.

Chantel didn't relax until she was in her place and the mournful whistle signaled they had left Boston. When she did, it was to find blood on her lower lip where she had driven her teeth into it to keep them steady.

Now she could look back to the city she had been born in, the only home she'd ever known. Her father's grave lay behind. The sun would just be stealing through the big elm's branches to throw patterns on the quiet spot. At the moment of departure, her courage failed. Had she done the right thing, going off like this? She had a wild urge to leap from her seat and shout, "Stop the train! It's all a mistake!" She desperately clutched the top of her carpetbag, feeling the reassuring presence of her Bible, and sank back deeper into the seat.

Boston lay behind. What was ahead? She

peered from the window, trying to see where she was being carried. All she could see was the horizon and storm clouds gathering in the train's path.

The first part of her journey was to remain forever obscured by mists of misery. Until they reached Chicago, Chantel paid little attention to the countryside through which she traveled. Every time the mournful whistle blew to announce town or crossing, its scream rang in her ears, "Go-o-o ba-a-ck." She carefully turned from the window, pulled her veil close about her in case Lydia and Arthur had mysteriously discovered her flight and wired ahead to stop her. If the conductor came through with orders to apprehend a fleeing madwoman, could she convince him she was sane?

Chantel spent much of her time reading her precious Bible, refusing to mingle with curious passengers who made overtures of friendship. Yet as the train ate mile after mile, she regained a sense of security and shyly smiled when spoken to. She also started watching the scenery pass by. If she never came back, it would be nice to know something of the country.

"It's so different from Boston!" she said aloud.

A rollicking laugh seconded her comment. "That it is."

Chantel spun her head from the window, her dark eyes wide in astonishment. She hadn't realized anyone had sat down next to her. Now merry blue eyes under a shock of graying hair sparkled with fun. "Mind if I sit here?"

"Not at all." Some of her instinctive distrust of strangers cooled the warm greeting she had almost given.

The lady didn't seem to mind. She settled her ample self more comfortably, straightened her long, well-worn skirts, and smiled again. "I'm S'rena Farley, and am I ever glad to be going home!"

Chantel couldn't resist the first friendly words she'd heard since leaving Boston. Besides, if anyone was looking for her, they'd never suspect a girl traveling with an older, responsible woman. "Your home is in the west?"

"Sure is. Montana Territory." A sunburst of wrinkles deepened around the laughing blue eyes and fresh pink cheeks. "I was one of those following her man to the gold fields. Lived through the Indian wars and hard times, then saved a bit and bought a little store after my man died."

Chantel looked at her companion in awe.

"You mean you actually fought Indians?" Fear filled her, and she clutched her Bible again. "There won't be any trouble now, will there?"

"Course not. They're all under treaty. You'll see lots of them, but not looking down the barrel of a rifle." A somber shadow darkened Serena's countenance.

Chantel pulled her cloak closer. Visions of Indians and raids raced through her ever-active brain. "You did that?"

"We had to." The simple words told Chantel of tragedy better than a long explanation could ever have done.

"Mrs. Farley, what is it like? Montana Territory, I mean." Chantel cast aside her reserve, determined to discover what her new home would be.

"Call me S'rena. Montana Territory folks aren't much on formality." She looked Chantel over, approval evident in the beaming face. "It's kind of like marriage: heaven to some, hell to others."

Chantel started violently and covered it with a cough. Her heart beat until she wondered if it could be heard. Had she been mistaken in grasping at a friendly smile? Had this woman somehow learned who she was? Another look at Serena dispelled her doubts. Only openness and honesty touched the middle-aged face with the young eyes that had seen so much.

"All you have to do in Montana Territory is travel apiece and if you don't like one kind of country, why, you'll soon be in another!"

Chantel joined in her rich laughter. "It sounds big."

"It is, and not just in space. It —" she broke off. "What's your name, child?"

Miss Evans trembled on Chantel's tongue. She rejected it immediately; it would be too unfriendly. "Chantel Evans."

"Chantel?" The genial face screwed into a question. "Seems like I've heard that before."

"You have?" Chantel leaned forward, unable to control her excitement.

Serena concentrated, then a wide white smile lit up her face. "I've got it. That's the little town, not much more than a trading post, near the Triangle C." Her eyes opened wider. "Evans. Are you related to Charles Evans?"

"You *know* him?"

"Honey, every man, woman, and child from the Bitterroots to Butte either knows or knows about Charles Evans. He's done more toward getting folks to think about becoming a state than anyone in that part of the country." She eyed Chantel. "How come you didn't know that?"

"We haven't been in close touch," Chantel confessed, a burning blush coloring her face. "There was a misunderstanding between my father and grandfather."

Serena discreetly changed the subject. "I heard Charles Evans speak once to a group of men in Butte. Your grandfather's a fine man."

The woman's praise lifted Chantel's spirits. "I can hardly wait to meet him, although he sends me a present every year."

"I haven't been to the Triangle C, but folks say it's one of the prettiest parts of Montana. I do know those narrow valleys are rich and the temperature is milder than other parts of the territory. The Chinook winds see to that."

"I never heard of a Chinook wind. Aren't all winds alike?"

The same throaty laugh Serena had issued earlier filled the air. "Not at all. Chinook is an Indian word for the warm, dry winds that come and clear the snow overnight. You can even smell them!"

"Your home doesn't happen to be near my grandfather's ranch does it?" Chantel wistfully asked. How wonderful it would be to have this good woman nearby.

"No." Serena shook her head. "I'm up by Missoula. Means 'by the chilling waters.' Maybe that grandfather of yours will bring you to see me someday."

Chantel blinked hard at the openhearted invitation. "I hope so." *If I stay that long,* she added silently.

The small towns gave way to the prairies of Nebraska and eastern Wyoming, but Chantel no longer looked over her shoulder to what was past. Serena Farley was a well of experiences. Chantel discovered she had developed an insatiable curiosity about the Montana Territory. She never tired of hearing Serena's tales. They were not always happy, although the covered wagon trek Serena and her husband had made to the gold fields had been joyful as well as hard work. But the two children carried off by Indians while Serena and her husband worked the fields less than a quarter mile away brought shadows to the lined face.

"I thought I'd go mad. I couldn't bear it! How could a loving God let such a thing happen?"

The familiar cry rang a responsive bell in Chantel's heart. She, too, had cried out asking why.

"Months later they were returned to us. Troops had attacked an Indian encampment and found the children but didn't know who they were. We heard white children had been found." Unashamed tears streamed down Serena's face. "I praised my Lord all those miles we rode to get them. They didn't know us at first, but when we got them home, little two-year-old Billy went right to his bed. We never let them out of sight again till Sally married and went back east to live. Billy and his wife live just across the street from me." She fell silent, hands clasped in an almost prayerful attitude. "It took me a long time to see how God let it happen." She raised one hand and wiped the tears away. "Now I know that because of it, I learned to appreciate my children as more than just mine and to see them as God's first of all."

Chantel's throat ached at the beauty of the story. "Do you believe there's a reason for everything that happens to us?"

"I do." The answer was uncompromising. "Usually it's to help bring us closer to our Lord. I know I was never so close to Jesus in my life as during those terrible months of waiting." Pure beauty shone in her eyes which looked like mountain lakes. "I knew He was there."

Chantel would never forget her first sight of the Rockies. She had awakened from a nap when Serena gently prodded her. "Don't sleep through some of the grandest scenery God ever created."

Chantel rubbed her eyes, then caught her breath.

Rearing thousands of feet into the blue, blue sky were mountains such as she had only seen in pictures. They started as rolling foothills, grew into pine, aspen, fir, and cottonwood slopes, then shot into towering, glistening, snow-clad peaks. Every adjective she had ever heard failed to describe their majesty.

" 'The fool hath said in his heart, There is no God.' " Serena's quotation was cut short as she glimpsed the reverence in Chantel's gaze. She sat back to feast her own eyes on the magnificent panorama ahead, content to allow Chantel the experience of the Rockies.

Crossing the continental divide, which Serena explained was where the waters divided to run east and west to the Atlantic and Pacific oceans through the rivers and streams, was exciting. Yet the strain accompanying Chantel's flight from Boston, coupled with the long trip, was extracting its price. Chantel was tired. Even the beautiful mountains and arriving at Ogden couldn't quite erase her dread of that first meeting with Grandfather Evans. She hoarded every bit and piece of information Serena gladly gave, storing it against that meeting.

"It's still a wild land," Serena warned, a motherly glint in her eyes. Although Chantel had been purposely vague about her reasons for coming to Montana Territory, she had told Serena about losing both mother and father, then briefly touched on Lydia and Anita, omitting all mention of Arthur Masters. If Serena caught overtones, she was too wise to show it. She continued, "There are always accidents on cattle ranches. Cowboys get trampled. Rustlers seem to multiply. The bigger the ranch, the more trouble with rustlers."

"Yet you say you wouldn't live anywhere else," Chantel marveled.

"I wouldn't." Serena's blue eyes snapped fire. "This country needs strong God-fearing men and stouthearted Christian wives and mothers. It's got its share of two-legged skunks, but there are decent, hard-working pioneers here who'll fight the storms for this land." Her indignation passed and she teased, "I predict some Montana cowboy will be building a cabin for you within a year."

"Oh, no!" Chantel drew back, hands out, as if to ward off the suggestion.

"Child, what's wrong?" Serena took Chantel's cold hands in her two warm ones.

Chantel tried to laugh but couldn't quite make it. "It's just that I — I don't think I'll ever marry."

"Is that all?" Serena's honest surprise was followed by a shrewd glance. "I s'pose some eastern varmint has soured you on men." The rich rose filling Chantel's face encouraged her. "You'd be surprised how quickly he'd be driven out of town out here for bothering a lady. Our cowboys may be a rough lot, but they respect womanhood. They may yell and shoot and fight and drink, but —"

Chantel was horrified. "You mean you *condone* all that? You think I could marry a ruffian?"

"Don't be absurd!" Serena's laugh tempered her quick retort. "Never marry any man who won't be more loyal to his Lord than even to you. I've known wild cowboys who met truehearted girls, settled down, and became Christian examples to their neighbors. Anyway," she chuckled, "if the Good Lord has a cowboy for you, you'll know it. Just don't be too quick to rush off after the first man who's nice to you."

"I won't." Chantel couldn't take offense at the loving advice. Every mile between Boston and Ogden had seared into her consciousness how she had done just what Serena warned about: painted glowing pictures of Arthur to herself in order to escape Lydia, instead of seeking her heavenly Father first.

"It's all so strange," she confessed to Serena once they had boarded the Utah and Northern for the last stage of their journey. They were traveling due north, through part of Idaho, headed toward Dillon. "I saw men actually carrying guns! I never saw anyone in Boston with a gun."

Serena's face was grim. "Out here a man never knows when he'll run into danger. Rattlesnakes, coyotes — it's best to be ready."

"Will I be in any danger on my grandfather's ranch? You called it the Triangle C. What does that mean?"

Serena gave her a keen look. "The most danger you'll be in is the danger of having some lovesick cowboy up and carry you off!" Her eyes rested on the lovely face above the fresh blouse Chantel had donned. When Chantel's dark eyes flashed, Serena patted her hand. "I'm teasing." She

76

drew paper and pencil from her purse. "You asked about the Triangle C. It's like this." She quickly drew a small picture. "Every rancher has a brand that is burned into his cattle to mark them as his. Several ranchers' cattle may graze together. When they round them up for marketing, they can be quickly separated." She pointed. "See? This ⟁c is your grandfather's brand."

Chantel gazed at the picture. "There's so much to learn! It's worse than when I studied French."

Serena just laughed. "Here are some other brands." She filled the page with symbols. "This ⊕ is the Cross O. Here's the Diamond X, ◈. And the Box K ⬚K⬚. Don't worry. You'll learn." She added slowly, "I just hope you'll be able to see under all the rawness and newness to this land as it really is."

"I'll try," Chantel promised, suddenly sober at thought of their coming parting.

"I wish I could see you clear to the Triangle C, but Billy will be waiting for me at the end of the line. He'd worry himself sick if I didn't get there on time."

A spurt of pride made Chantel answer, "I'll be all right. Surely there will be a stage to Chantel."

"Not likely." Serena's practicality doused

Chantel's hopes. "You'll need to get a place to stay and send word you're at Dillon, or hire someone to drive you to the ranch." A frown marred her forehead. "You said your grandfather didn't know you were coming? Too bad. He'd have been there to meet you."

"I left in a hurry," was the best Chantel could muster. She deliberately changed the subject. "How will you get to Missoula?"

"Billy's team. He has a pair of quick-steppers and is anxious to try them out."

The train pulled into Dillon, whistle shrieking. Chantel stepped to the platform, aware of Serena still on the lowest step. "Good-bye!"

"God bless, child."

The train snorted, belched, and spit out a cloud of black smoke. Chantel hastily stepped back as it chugged away, gathering speed. Serena became a waving miniature, then only a dot, and at last Chantel turned to survey her surroundings.

The tiny station was like many other stations she had seen. The agent was busy checking baggage. She saw her trunk in a far corner and relaxed. The box of books had also been unloaded.

There were loungers here, too: booted, spurred men with wide hats and bright handkerchiefs around their necks. Some wore the woolly outside trousers Serena had called chaps. There were other differences. Even though the cowboys looked at her, she saw none of the insolent appraisal that had been in the eyes of the men in the Boston station. When one of the cowboys caught her eye and she lifted her chin, he turned red as a schoolgirl.

Reassured, she turned to the agent, a weatherbeaten man with leathery cheeks and calloused fingers. "I wonder if you might tell me the best way to get to the Triangle C?"

He stared so long that she flushed. Hadn't he understood? She knew her speech was far different from the western drawls she had encountered in her travels, especially after they crossed the Rockies. She tried again. "Please, is there a conveyance I could hire to take me to the Triangle C?"

Deadly silence greeted her question. Not only the agent seemed stricken dumb, every sign of movement among the nearby cowboys halted.

Chantel ignored the warning signals creeping along her nerves, telling her something must be terribly wrong. These men appeared of at least average intelligence. What was the matter, that they did not answer? Perhaps they were indulging in some kind of joke. Serena had warned her not to be taken in by cowboy pranks. "They are like a bunch of small boys let out of school," she said. "They dearly love playing tricks. You're new, and they'll want your attention. You'll be a tenderfoot, but don't let them get the best of you — and don't hold it against them."

A spurt of anger drew her shoulders back, chilled her eyes to dark pools. She started to speak, remembered a story she once read about westerners who teased a schoolteacher, and thought better of flaring out and accusing them of inhospitality. If she could get no answer here, she would go elsewhere. She had spied a log building a little way down the street. Hating the dust, she stepped off the crude boardwalk and skirted the group of cowboys, holding her skirts up as best she could with one hand. Her carpetbag and reticule weighed heavily on the other.

"Aw, someone better tell her."

Chantel turned toward the speaker, eyes blazing. So it had been a trick! She faced the cowboy, who had blushed. "Tell me what?" Little shreds of ice frosted her words.

His honest eyes met hers. She couldn't discern what was there — sympathy, admiration, or a combination? He doffed his big hat.

"Well?"

He scuffed his boot toe in the dust. "Why were you askin' about gettin' to the Triangle C?"

Chantel measured every word. "Not that I consider it any of your affair, but Charles Evans happens to be my grandfather."

The cowboy's face went from dusky red to pale under his tan. Something in his dark eyes winged its way to Chantel as he said softly, "I'm sorry to hear that, miss. Evans is — isn't well."

"What's wrong with him?" Chantel held her breath.

The speaker's eyes turned hard. "He got himself a case of lead poisoning."

"Impossible!" Chantel gasped. "How on earth . . ."

Sympathy crowded out everything else in the man's soft, dark gaze. "Seems there was a run-in with rustlers. When it was over, the ranch hands found Evans facedown by the stream. Not dead, but with a bullet hole in him." He kept his steady eyes on her dead-white face. "That's why when you asked about gettin' to the ranch nobody answered."

PART II

5

Brandon Morgan reined in Dark Star on top of the rise. The black mare snorted, breathing hard. The climb from the valley to the pine-dotted bluff was a hard one, requiring a rider's steady nerve and, in places, delicate guidance over the narrow trail.

As always, Brand's love for his ranch filled him. From his vantage point he could see for miles. They all belonged to him. Hundreds of acres encompassing grazing land, forests, winding streams, and to the west, the Bitterroot range.

"We've come a long way, old girl." The ungloved hand stroking the horse was as tan as the skin drawn taut over his high cheekbones. "Not many men at thirty can claim this."

Dark Star whinnied and pranced.

"I reckon folks'd think I'd been eating loco weed, hearing me talk to a horse." Brand dismounted and threw the reins over his horse's head. "But you're better company than most men and the only female I ever saw that could be trusted." Dark Star, trained to stand when the reins were down, rolled liquid eyes toward her master and daintily moved her head to a particularly tempting patch of grass.

Brand chuckled, unscrewed the top of his canteen, and drank deeply. Dark Star got her share from her master's strong, cupped hand, then Brand tossed his well-worn Stetson aside and emptied the canteen over his tawny head, shaking himself like a shaggy horse to get rid of the drops. There was something satisfying about the wetness. Although it was still morning, the sun shone warmly, highlighting the valley and the Rocking M.

He scanned the panoramic scene before him, noting with clear amber eyes the slowly moving cattle dotted with even more slowly moving cowboys. Off to one side of the valley, the roof of his home was a dark patch. The bunkhouse and corrals were hidden by clumps of cottonwoods. As he swiveled toward the east, he clenched his hands into fists and swore.

One tiny curl of smoke had risen above the bench separating the Rocking M from Evans's Triangle C.

Brand vaulted to Dark Star's back. "Too far away for the boys to try and alert them." Dark Star was already picking her way back over the trail, which needed repair. "It may just be a rider wanting a hot cup of coffee. Or —" he hitched his gun belt a little higher, "maybe we'll catch a two-bit rustler."

Hating the delay, but mindful of Dark Star's welfare, he gave her time to reach open prairie before he shouted in her ear. She stretched out and ran, sailing over clumps of sagebrush and coming down, only to rise again in perfect cadence. Even through his preoccupation with what was on the far side of the bench, Brand felt exultant at Dark Star's wild, free stride.

Just before he reached the top, he reined her in. "Stand," he ordered in a low voice. She obeyed without a nicker.

Placing one foot directly behind the other, as an Indian walks, Brand stole through the cottonwoods. It was as he suspected: Whoever built that fire was mighty close to Bannock Creek, which separated the Triangle C from the Rocking M.

He came to the edge of the thicket, drew his Colt revolver, and parted the bushes in front of him. A grim smile creased his face. "Hands up!" He stepped from his shelter toward the curiously frozen figure half-bent over a bawling calf.

"Drop the iron and turn around." Brand's voice was deadly persuasive. "And don't reach for your gun, or I'll put a hole in you."

The branding iron clattered to the ground and the calf galloped away, still bawling. The overalled cowboy turned, spurs clinking.

"You!" A world of disgust lay in the spat-out word.

"Hello, Brand." Duke Price started to lower his hands.

"Keep them up," Brand ordered, striding closer. A flip of his left hand sent Duke's six-shooter flying. "Well?"

Duke's slim face never moved a muscle.

"I asked you a question." Brand's steely eyes never left his former partner's face. "Can you give me one good reason I shouldn't string you up right here?"

"None except your own judgment." Dark eyes clashed with amber.

"Judgment! What more evidence do I need than this?" Brand roared, pointing at the fire and branding iron. He sheathed his Colt and picked up the iron. "Clever. Very clever." He shoved it into the sand, leaving an imprint. "So this is how the Circle Four Peaks operates." He traced a Rocking M in the sand, then stamped the branding iron over it. It instantly changed from M to $\text{\textcircled{MM}}$.

"I'm not stealing from you, Firebrand."

If the nickname registered, Brand didn't show it. He merely laughed, showing teeth that made him look like a tawny mountain lion. "From where I stand, it sure looks like it." Fire and ice flowed in his veins. "You'll remember we parted company a year ago because I didn't like some of the talk in town about you. You never bothered to deny it." A vein stood out in his forehead. "Little stories about you being seen with certain drifters right before cattle started disappearing." His lips curled. "You didn't have an explanation then, either."

He abruptly abandoned his accusation. "Why, Duke?" He was totally unprepared for the other's reply.

"I can't tell you."

Brand could feel the blood sing in his head. "Get off my land. This is the second warning. If I ever catch you here again, so help me, I'll —" Sheer fury choked off his threat. "Get your horse and ride. If it weren't for the years we've been friends, I'd shoot you like the rotten rustler you are."

Duke's face gleamed as he mounted the bay nearby. "I'm no more a rustler than you are. Someday you'll know that." The clatter of hooves drowned out his voice as he disappeared through the cottonwoods.

Brand stared after him, puzzled. There had been the ring of truth in Duke's voice. Years of being friends had given Brand the ability to tell when Duke was lying. Yet if he wasn't rustling, why wouldn't he talk straight?

"He must be protecting someone." His suspicion crystallized. "Even when we split and he took over the Circle Four Peaks." The idea rankled. "Some loyalty! Throwing me down for some cattle thief." Saying it out loud made it seem even worse. Brand's jaw set as he carried water from Bannock Creek and doused the fire, stamping out every bit and scattering the wet, charred remains.

Yet he could not get away from his thoughts. He whistled for Dark Star and slowly rode back to the ranch house, troubled. Had he done wrong in letting Duke go? What was to prevent him from sneaking in and driving off a bunch of steers some stormy night when they were already restless? Tortured by old ties warring with what lay ahead, he made a hard decision. He took care of Dark Star, pried a hearty meal out of his Chinese cook, Ah Soong, and on a fresh mount, headed for the Triangle C.

Indian Paintbrush and sagebrush swayed in the breeze. It was the kind of day Brand loved best. A man could be out doing when the smiling land beckoned. In the distance mountains of silver-touched clouds banked the horizon. Brand loved them, too; they carried both the threat and promise of storm. A slicker always lay ready in his saddlebags. Many was the time he'd been caught out, riding ahead of sweeping storms that deluged the country, leaving swollen streams and raging rivers.

By the time Brand reached the Triangle C, some of his earlier mood had vanished. Without telling Charles Evans about Duke, he'd see if the Triangle C had lost more cattle. With herds the size the two ranches ran, it wasn't easy to tell, but Charles might have noticed something funny going on.

Brand unconsciously stroked the fine scar that ran from his eyebrow to his hairline. He'd been pitched from a horse while still a kid.

"Charles's kind of like the dad I left buried back in Virginia," he soliloquized, absently straightening his shoulders. "Always listens before he decides." He grinned a bit ruefully. "Guess old Firebrand Morgan could do better to imitate him." He grunted in distaste as he passed Chantel, a place too small to be dignified by calling it a town: one big store, a few scattered houses, a well. It had been named for Charles Evans's long-dead wife, and there was an eastern granddaughter with that name, too. The old man's only son had headed east and never came back. Scorn lifted Brand's head. Why any man'd want to live back there he didn't know. Yet if his own father hadn't died in the Civil War and his heartbroken mother a few years later, would he ever have come to Montana Territory?

"I'm glad I did," he told the crumpled hills and gathered clouds, leaving Chantel behind. A half-mile down the road, he jerked the bay to a standstill. Where only rolling land had been at the edge of the Circle Four Peaks, a half-completed building now stood. Peeled pine logs were being fitted into place by a half-dozen workmen.

"What do you think you're doing?"

A swarthy man eyed him and spat tobacco juice on the ground. "We're buildin' the Chantel Saloon."

"Evans will never stand for that," Brand told the hostile man.

Raucous laughter shattered the peaceful day. "That's why we're buildin' it here. Ain't on the old man's land. This's Duke Price's spread, case you forgot." He spat again. "Reckon the cowboys around here ain't above havin' a place to get a drink and play a hand of cards." He winked at another man as repulsive as himself. "Might even bring in some ladies, if you know what I mean."

Too disgusted to answer, Brand swung his horse back to the road. So Duke was now promoting what was bound to become a hellhole, and on his own land next to Chantel! What was Charles going to say?

Charles Evans had plenty to say. His great fist crashed down on the handmade carved table and rattled the coffee cups his Irish housekeeper, Molly McLeod, had brought in. "I've a notion to send the boys over to pull the thing down." Eyes as gray as his hair shot sparks. "I'll be hanged if I'll let that kind of thing come in and interfere with everything I've taken years to build!" He impaled Brand with a glance. "What's gotten into Duke Price? Ever since you and he split up, I've been hearing things."

"I don't know." Brand scowled, wondering how much to say. "I can't figure if someone's got a hold on him, or what. He refused to give one word of reason for the strange way he was acting when we went our separate ways. Since then," he shrugged, "I don't think things are any better. Now he's building this so-called saloon right where it's bound to cause trouble. Makes me wonder what next."

Charles's keen eyes twinkled. "Whatever it is, you'll handle it. Duke ain't the only one folks talk about. Seems I've heard tall tales about one Firebrand Morgan on occasion."

"Tall tales is just what they are," Brand assured him with a grin. "Don't believe everything you hear."

"Maybe we'd better remember that about Duke." Charles didn't give Brand a chance to speak. "Bunk here tonight, boy, and we'll get up a game of poker. Santa Fe and the boys'll be back in after supper."

"When's Santa Fe going to marry that housekeeper of yours? He's been mooning around ever since McLeod got tromped by a horse, and that was two years ago." A vision of the grizzled foreman brought an accompanying laugh. "Never knew any man to be so set on a woman as he is on her."

"It'd be a mighty good match for both of them." The gray eyes twinkled again. "Since you're so danged interested in them getting married, when are you going to take the leap?"

"Not me." Brand drummed his fingers on the table. "No filly's going to get her brand on me."

"It's worth it, if you get the right one."

Brand couldn't believe his ears. "You, advising me to get hitched? After telling me all this time you'd never get married again?"

Something in the old man's face stilled Brand, and his quiet comment, "I won't. I had everything a man could hope for the first time," opened a door to Charles that had been closed and bolted until then. "She gave me love and a son."

"Who left you." Brand regretted it the minute he said it.

Charles's face sagged. "Yes. But it was better to have had a son who did what he felt right than never to have had one at all."

Not because he cared, but to avoid the pain in his friend's face, Brand asked, "His daughter must be about grown now, isn't she?"

Charles brightened. "Yes. She'll be

twenty-one in October. She always sends a little note every year thanking me for whatever present I get Molly to send." He riffled a stack of letters and magazines on his desk, then held out a small picture. "This was her when she was eighteen."

"Pretty."

Charles didn't seem to notice his lack of interest. "She's good, too. I can tell by her letters. Haven't heard for a long time now, but I suppose she's being followed by half the boys in Boston. If she's half the girl her grandmother was, she'll show her French blood." He put the picture back on his desk. "Let's mosey down to the bunkhouse and scare up some of the boys. I heard them come awhile ago, and they should be through with supper."

Their plans for a card game never materialized. Before they got across the yard to the bunkhouse, Santa Fe Jones, bloody bandage wound around his head, rode into the yard, reeling in the saddle. "Rustlers. West range." He slid from the horse into Brand's strong arms.

"Molly!" Charles roared, kicking open the hewn log door to the house. "Bring hot water and clean cloths." He motioned Brand to the blanket-covered couch by the fireplace. "Put him there."

Brand obeyed. If he hadn't let Duke go free, would this have happened? He dropped to his knees. "Where were you?" he demanded hoarsely.

Santa Fe opened his eyes. "Over by where they're building that —" he jerked his head, and a spasm of pain crossed his face as he sank back on the couch.

Brand was already halfway to the door when Charles barked, "Wait! We'll get the boys."

There was no need. Santa Fe's dramatic return had been seen by the hands, who spilled out the bunkhouse door and were already saddling horses. Moments later a band of relentless men rode down the way Brand had traveled that afternoon. Once someone asked, "Anyone got a rope?" A clear picture of Duke Price rose in Brand's mind, and he was glad to hear Charles growl, "No ropes. If we get the man who shot Santa Fe, he's going to stand trial — and talk. We're going to find out who's behind this." His flat statement sent trickles of fear down Brand's erect spine. "No matter who it is."

By the time they reached the nearly completed saloon, the storm clouds Brand had seen earlier fulfilled their promise. "Can't track in this," he muttered. "Shall we ride straight in to the Circle Four Peaks?"

"We can't prove a thing." Charles sounded defeated. "But I have a plan." He outlined it to Brand as they battled the driving rain on the way home. "Just let it be known in certain quarters."

The following morning Brand deliberately stopped by the new structure on his way back to the Rocking M.

"Hey," he called to the man who'd been so insolent the day before. "You see anybody riding fast through here last night about suppertime?"

The man was surly. "So what if he did?"

"Someone shot Santa Fe Jones."

"That so? Now ain't that too bad?"

Brand wanted to smash his ugly face but only said, "Whoever did it better keep right on riding."

"Santa Fe gonna croak?"

"He might. If he does, someone in these parts will hang for murder." He caught the startled glance the bully gave his partner. "Old man Evans ain't telling all he knows." He added casually, "Wouldn't surprise me if Santa Fe already told who shot him."

"Got nothin' to do with us," the man growled.

"So long." Brand touched the bay's

flanks with his heels, well pleased with the reaction he'd seen when he faithfully carried out Charles's orders.

Two days later, every bit of satisfaction vanished when a rider from the Triangle C burst into Brand's living room. "Come quick! The old man's hurt bad. Shot. Didn't spend last night at home, and this mornin' a bunch of us found him face down by Bannock Creek, a bullet in his back."

"Has anyone sent for Doc?" Brand was already out the door, whistling for Dark Star. He grabbed his saddle and was ready when she came.

"Yup. Molly sent me for you before Doc got there." The young cowboy gulped. "He'd bled an awful lot."

Brand thought for one awful moment that he would pitch from the saddle. He gritted his teeth and called to Dark Star. With a giant leap she left the Triangle C rider behind, but Brand couldn't run away from the feeling that it was his fault.

"Well, Doc?"

The grim-faced physician looked Brand straight in the eye. "I got the bullet out and cleaned the hole. It went through. Shouldn't be any infection. Molly'll keep it tended to."

"Then he'll be all right?"

"I didn't say that." The beetling brows met. "He lay there no one knows how long and lost a lot of blood."

Anger at the bushwacker licked at Brand. "Did he see who shot him?"

"No. He said he heard a rustle in the cottonwoods then felt something hit him. Blacked out and didn't come to until the boys came." Doc stiffly walked toward the door. "I'll be back out tomorrow. Molly can handle everything for now." He paused. "Young man, I'd suggest you stick around here if you can. Somebody appears to have a powerful grudge against the Triangle C." The door banged behind him.

Brand stopped to remove his clinking spurs before knocking on the door of the sickroom. Molly's white face peeked out. She motioned him in but laid a finger across her lips.

Brand had to blink to keep back the first tears he'd felt since his mother died. Charles Evans lay so still and white that he no longer resembled the healthy rancher who had ridden out after Santa Fe's enemy a few days earlier. Grim determination to catch and punish whomever was responsible rose in Brand until he thought he would choke. The look in his face stopped

Molly from speaking, and she wordlessly held open the door.

For three days Charles lay as if dead but on the fourth morning he roused and looked straight into the amber eyes that had watched over him every minute that Molly was not there.

"Don't talk," Brand warned. "You were shot. You're going to be all right, but you have to rest."

Something shivered in the depths of his eyes, but Charles obediently closed his eyes. Brand heard stirring and turned to meet Molly's look. "Thank God," she whispered.

Brand looked at her with unutterable scorn. *Just like a woman.* Molly was a pretty good sort, but she was just like all the rest, thanking God for the fact that Charles was strong enough to overcome his wound. Where had God been when the yellow skunk who shot him in the back and left him for dead crawled away, rejoicing over his attack? Why thank God now, when the danger certainly wasn't over?

Brand's lips set in a harsh, cold line. If there had ever been a God, He must have ridden off to some other range. He couldn't have been around recently to let the finest man in Montana Territory be cut down by a killer. He hadn't been around to save Brand's father, either, in spite of the prayers Brand knew his mother had offered all during the war. Or even after the hesitant prayers the boy Brand had once stumblingly said. Since God had so conveniently been off somewhere picking flowers when He was needed, He needn't think He was going to get credit now, no matter what Molly McLeod believed.

6

Anxious days gave way to hope. Molly McLeod frankly praised God. Brand lifted one eyebrow and rejoiced in the clean living and superb health that was gradually bringing Charles back from the borderline of death. Brand had put the Rocking M into the capable hands of his foreman, Carson, and stayed with Charles. "Needed a vacation, anyway," he grinned at the invalid one day, noticing color in the drawn face against the pillows.

"Reckon I'm too ornery to die." Charles fixed his gray eyes on Brand but was interrupted by an indignant Molly. Her eyes snapped as she brushed a stray lock of auburn hair from her round face. "Seems to me you'd better be thankin' your Maker, Mr. Evans, instead of acting like you've done something great on your own!" She flounced out, irritation in every line of her straight back.

"She's right, you know."

Brand slopped coffee into his saucer, amazed at the look of shame in the thin face opposite. "You *believe* that?"

"I used to." Charles sighed, and the light went from his eyes. "Somewhere along the way — after losing my wife and having Charles, Jr. go back east — I got to thinking God was picking on me." Restless fingers, strangely out of place on the white spread, drummed a tattoo against his cup. "Since I've been laid up I've had time to do another kind of thinking. What've I ever done for God?"

"You've done a lot for Montana Territory," Brand protested, annoyance coloring his voice. "You've ridden straight and helped others get started, like me."

"It ain't enough, Brand. What good is it all going to be when I have to leave it, unless along the way I've been more than just a good man?"

Brand sprang to his feet with catlike grace, his eyes blazing. "Even if there was a God, what more could He want from a man than to be a square shooter?" He managed a laugh from the churning anger inside that had never subsided after his parents died. "What kind of God would ask more? Seems to me that'd be enough to get us cowpokes a chance to drag our spurs over those golden streets I've heard preachers rave about."

"Not in a million sunsets."

"How can you be so sure?" Brand's breath came in quick little puffs.

"I've never been surer of anything on this earth." Sincerity poured from the old man's face. "I may not have lived up to it, but I know what God wants. We've got to see ourselves as sinners and accept His Son's death and resurrection as a free gift." Charles leaned forward, his eyes intent. "Suppose you were about to be hung for rustling and along came a cowboy who took your place, dying so you'd be free? How would you feel about it?"

Brand whitened. "I'd be a pretty miserable cuss if I didn't stop him."

"Suppose you couldn't stop him? What if he'd gone ahead and done it before you even knew what he was planning?"

Brand's eyes stung the way they had once when he'd been caught in a sandstorm, but he couldn't answer.

The persuasive voice went on. "A feller'd have to be downright ornery to not be thankful, wouldn't he?" A waterhole of silence fell between them. "That's what I've been doing, Brand."

Brand whipped around to look out the window, awed by the reverence he'd heard, which was so far removed from the old man's usual bellow.

Charles lay still, eyes fixed on the far wall. "No more. I've talked it over with Him and asked if His Son couldn't be my pard from here on out."

Brand took one quick step toward the bed. "You aren't feeling bad again?"

The hearty laugh reassured him. "Nope. This isn't a bid to get in good before I go." His gray eyes twinkled. "Doc says I can get up tomorrow. It was worth being shot to have to look at myself and see part of me was missing. Someday you'll feel the same."

"Never!" Brand snapped. "I leave God be and He does the same for me, if there even is a God." To his relief, Charles changed the subject and they chatted amiably until dusk fell. Then Brand said, "Since you're so all-fired ready to crawl out of the bunk, I'll ride on home."

The moon sat on a low rise like a giant yellow face as Brand rode slowly home, letting Dark Star pick her way. Some of the worry melted inside, leaving him tired. He could do with a good night's sleep! Even Molly didn't know of the nights he'd paced his room after she relieved him by the sickbed. He was used to death: Life in this country was uncertain, always ready to strike when most unexpected. But to lose Charles! Brand shoved the thought rudely aside, shaking himself impatiently. The old man was getting well. He'd gone a little soft from the accident, but at least he was improving.

Brand grunted, and Dark Star pricked up her ears. "It's okay, Star. Just wondering about Charles. Religion's never seemed to be in his line." His voice sounded unexpectedly loud in the pure air. The moon had left its resting place and risen to dump light over the ground. Far in the distance Brand could hear a calf bawling for its mother, then the short, sharp bark of a coyote — sounds as familiar as his own voice. He filled his lungs with air, rejoicing in the clean smell faintly tinged with sage. What a night! Instead of his senses being dulled, they had been sharpened by his vigil. A man couldn't ask more than a night like this and a good horse under him.

Yet as mile gave way to lonely mile, an odd sense of loss touched him. He hadn't taken on another pard after he and Duke split. Regret rode with him. Unbidden memories of nights on the prairie, camp-fires beneath a big rock, sleeping in the timber came, always with the image of a dark-haired laughing man. If only Duke hadn't gone wrong! Or if he had explained the gossip. Try as he would, Brand hadn't been able to open up to anyone since. His boys were always glad to see him, but none could take Duke's place.

"I asked if His Son couldn't be my pard."

Charles's confession sent shivers up Brand's spine. His harsh laugh made Dark Star prance, and he patted her mane soothingly. "Can you imagine Jesus Christ being our pard, Star? He wouldn't even if I wanted Him, and I don't. A feller'd have to cut out all the cuss words he knew and start saying prayers." He laughed again, deliberately denying the tiny feeling of panic inside him. He was getting spooked as badly as Charles, what with the silver night and silent trails.

When he passed Chantel, he heard raucous music. The new building had been completed during his stay at the Triangle C. His brows drew together. The last thing they needed was this. He was tempted to fire a few shots in the air as he rode by, just to vent his disgust, but decided against it. When he saw Duke again, he'd tell him how rotten it was to bring in the kind of people who ran such places.

By the time he got home, every thought had been obliterated except the need for sleep. He stumbled to his bedroom, shed his clothes, and dropped into a stupor. Even his matchless health couldn't stand long days and nights without rest. Minutes or hours later he woke to a lamp shining in his eyes. His foreman, Carson, was shaking him.

"What?"

"Wake up, Brand." Another hard shake. "There's the devil to pay."

The drawn countenance of his trusted foreman chased away sleep. Brand was reaching for his clothes and boots even as he asked, "What's wrong?" Fear gripped him. "Not Evans?"

"Not exactly." Carson's face was shadowed by his ten-gallon hat. "Rosy here," he jerked one finger at the younger cowboy behind him, "rode in from Dillon. Don't know if he should tell the old man, on account of him bein' shot up and all."

"Tell him what?" Brand recognized one of the Triangle C hands, nicknamed Rosy for his habit of changing color easily. "Just what's going on?"

The cowboy, little more than a strapling, coughed. "It's the girl."

"Girl!" Brand stopped in the middle of buckling on his gun belt. "You got me out of bed in the middle of the night about a *girl?*" Hot anger poured through him. "You're the biggest idiot I've ever seen." Disgust closed his lips as he tossed the gun belt aside.

"But she says she's the old man's granddaughter!" Rosy reluctantly stepped forward, eyes bulging.

"What?"

"That's what she said." The cowboy stood his ground. "We'd all ridden in and were waiting when the train came in. This girl — lady —" he swallowed. "Anyway, she stepped down. We could see she wasn't from around here. I guess we all stared. She looked us over, cool as January, and asked the station agent how to get to the Triangle C."

"And?"

"And no one said anything. She asked again and then started down the street, goin' to the store, I guess. I felt sorry for her and said someone better tell her." He gulped. "She fixed great big black eyes on me and wanted to know what I meant."

A wave of color filled the boyish face. "When I asked how come she wanted to get to the Triangle C, she said she allowed it wasn't none of my business, but Charles Evans was her granddad."

"Well?" Brand's terse question brought another rush of color to Rosy's face.

"I had to tell her the old man'd been shot and was bad off."

Carson snorted. "You really *are* an idiot!"

"She asked." Rosy defended himself. "What was I s'posed to do?"

"Forget it." Brand fixed the cowboy with a cold stare. "What did she do?"

"Turned awful pale. I thought for a minute she might keel over, but she grabbed the hitching rail real hard and finally said, 'How can I get there?' The agent told her she better stay overnight, since it was so far to the Triangle C. First off I thought she was going to argue, but she finally gave in. The agent's going to try and get someone to fetch her out to the ranch in the morning." A surprising look of maturity settled on the boy's features. "Don't seem right to have her hauled out here by just anyone, so I rode hard."

"And you expect me to go get her?"

"She's the old man's kin." The boy's eyes were steady. "And seeing as how close you are, I thought —"

"Maybe she isn't even related. Maybe she heard the old man's about to cash in and decided to pose as his granddaughter and make some loot," Brand suggested.

Rosy's lips set stubbornly. "She's real. Dark and slim and ladylike." He turned. "If you don't want to go, I'll go back and bring her out myself."

Amusement tempered Brand's exasperation. "I'll go get her." He buckled his gun belt. "Carson, hitch up the team. Fool eastern girl probably never saw a horse."

Twenty minutes later, he was on his way to Dillon. It would be cutting it close, but he should get there before she took off with someone for the ranch. By dawn he was within a few miles of town, and sunup saw him rubbing down the horses and watering them before the long trip home.

The dark hours had not improved his temper. Even if she was Charles's long-lost granddaughter, she was a vulture. It was just too farfetched to believe she had happened to decide on a visit when the old man was ready to die. She'd probably heard somehow of the shooting and pretended to be surprised when Rosy told her so she could worm her way into the Triangle C spread. It was worth a lot. By the time he strode down the dusty street of Dillon, she was tried and convicted as a schemer.

It didn't help Brand's temper to find out from the station agent that she had spent the night at his home and he'd made arrangements for her to be taken to the Triangle C. "Why, you must have barely missed them!" the agent exclaimed. "They left here not more than ten minutes ago." He pointed west, where a slight cloud of dust verified his statement.

"I was rubbing down the horses." Brand started back down the street, his mood growing worse by the minute. A new thought stopped him. "Who took her?"

"Duke Price was on his way home. Said he'd be glad to drop her off. She's a nice little thing. Duke looked real pleased to have her setting alongside him."

"I'll bet he did," Brand snorted between his teeth. "Thanks."

He'd never made a faster job of hitching up the team. There was a shortcut between Dillon and the first stream. It was rough, but he should be able to cut them off there. Even if she was a conniving little schemer, she wasn't going to be taken home by Duke Price.

His horses were lathered by the time they reached the stream. He freed them and allowed them to graze the lush grass by the water's edge. The water was clear, so no one had crossed that morning. A few minutes later, a light rig slowly rounded the bend. Brand could see the slim, dark-clad figure of a girl perched next to Duke.

He forced a smile and stepped into the road. "Morning, Duke. Thanks for bringing Miss Evans this far. I'll take over now." He was so intent on Duke's set jaw that he barely heard the girl's gasp.

"I always finish what I start, Firebrand." Duke pulled up his team.

"Not this time." Brand walked to the rig. "The old man wants me to fetch his grand-daughter." Their eyes clashed until a soft voice inquired, "Mr. Price, who is this man?"

"May I present Brandon Morgan, ma'am." Duke's natural chivalry came to the rescue.

"My grandfather sent you to meet me?" Doubtful eyes dark as patches beneath rocks surveyed Brand. "He didn't know I was coming."

"Rosy rode out and told us." Brand hated to lie and salved his conscience by telling himself he really hadn't lied. If Charles had known she was in Dillon, he would have sent Brand.

Her voice quavered. "Then I'd better go with you." She started to clamber down, but Brand reached her and swung her easily to the ground.

"Thank you," she called over her shoulder as Duke finished lifting her box of books into the Rocking M buckboard.

"May I come see you?"

"Why," her eyes widened and a little smile tilted her mouth upwards, "I suppose so." Duke was still standing there as they drove away.

Brand grimly shut his lips in a straight line and concentrated on driving. So she wasn't just a schemer but also a flirt. In Dillon not even a full twenty-four hours, and already making arrangements for Duke to call. A real fast worker, this granddaughter from the east.

"Mr. Morgan, how is my grandfather?" Her question brought out all his resentment. "He's going to live, unfortunately for you."

"How dare you!"

He hadn't known eyes could blaze like that. Twin spots of color against her white skin showed her anger. He forced an amused laugh. "Really, Miss Evans, there's no need to play games with me. After all this time you show up here when the old man's conveniently been shot. I don't know how you discovered it, but it looked like a winning hand, didn't it? Long-lost granddaughter appears, charms rancher, winds up owning one of the finest ranches in western Montana."

"You think that of me?"

He took time to appreciate how well-done her simulated horror was before replying. "When put into words, it isn't very pretty, is it? But then, schemers seldom expect others to see through their little plans. Well, let me tell you one thing: You aren't going to do anything to upset Charles. He's on the mend, but that doesn't mean he can't suffer a setback. If I catch you doing anything to make that happen, you'll answer to me. Is that clear?"

"Perfectly. It's also clear to me that you say whatever comes into your head, so there's no use trying to change your mind."

"None whatsoever." That effectively cut off their conversation.

Miles later Brand pulled into the shade of some low-growing trees to the right of the road. "We'll rest here. Sorry I didn't have time to rustle any grub, but you can have a drink of water."

Black-velvet eyes stared haughtily down at him. "Grub? Oh, you mean lunch? The agent's wife packed a lunch." She motioned to a wrapped package. "I really don't care to eat. I just want to rest."

"Let me help you." He reached up to her.

"That is totally unnecessary." She started to swing down, but her skirt caught, and she fell into his arms. For the space of a heartbeat he held her, looking into her pale face, her wide, dark eyes glaring into his own. A pang went through him. In spite of her slim height, she seemed frail. Had he misjudged her? There were dark shadows of weariness beneath her eyes, as if she had not slept.

The next instant she struggled free and marched to the edge of the trickle of cold water leaping down the hillside. He watched her bathe her face and noted the sunlight playing in her raven-black hair. Rosy was right: She was pretty — the prettiest thing he'd seen in ages.

"Eat." He handed her the package. "I won't be slowed down by a fool girl who refuses to eat and will have to stop and rest every mile between here and the Triangle C."

A scornful look was his answer, but she accepted the cold biscuit and beef and ate daintily, then drank the water he brought her in the canteen.

"How much farther?" she asked wearily when they started again. He noticed how her eyes roved the country from low mesa to distant mountains and reluctantly admitted she at least had the sense to appreciate their beauty.

"About twelve miles."

"Twelve miles! But the Boston station agent figured it couldn't be over twenty miles from Dillon."

"Easterners don't know how far a Montana Territory mile stretches," he told her dryly, pointing to a butte ahead. "How far do you think that is from here?"

"A mile? two?" She sounded doubtful.

"Twenty miles." He glanced her way and caught the look in her face. "If you stick around these parts and ever go riding by yourself, which you shouldn't, remember that distances out here are deceiving." Curiosity prompted him to add, "You won't be staying long, I don't suppose."

Cool, remote eyes scanned him. "That depends on my grandfather."

With Charles's new softness, that could be quite a spell, Brand told himself bitterly. She was even more beautiful than the picture Charles had showed him. The old man'd never believe she was a vulture. It was even hard for him to believe it when he looked into her eyes. How could anyone who connived have such an innocent look? Or was that the way she meant to get by with it, by looking charming and innocent?

"Why did you come here?" he demanded rudely. "There's nothing to hold you here. You, an easterner! I suppose you'll hang around until the old man names you his heir, then trot back home."

Never had he seen sadness such as flashed across her face. He had to bend low to catch her whispered words. "No. I won't go back. I have no home. It really doesn't matter what you think of me. I just want to see my grandfather."

Brand was almost convinced he had been wrong. Perhaps her visit was one of those strange, unexplainable things that happened. Yet the next moment his tentative misgivings were turned to granite. She raised her head and looked across the valley to where a spot of color showed the carved-out setting for the Triangle C and said, "I want a home more than anything else in the world, and this is the only place I can find it."

He had been right. All the softness and appeal were merely weapons. Triangle C was what she wanted, and knowing Charles as Brand did, the Triangle C was exactly what she would get. The very fact she had left Boston to come to Montana Territory would sway any judgment Charles might have had. Brand iced over at the determination in her voice. Would his old friend be able to resist that dedicated look? It was up to Brand to see that he did.

7

Chantel gritted her teeth to keep from bursting into sobs. Why should she let this perfectly odious man beside her see into her heart? It had been bad enough to have to face the possible death of her grandfather, who was dear to her because of his likeness to her father. She had lain sleepless in the narrow cot the kindly station agent's wife had given her, haunted by fear, kept awake by every raucous laugh or beat of horses' hooves in the street. "Dear God," she had prayed into the terror of night after a long wail left her trembling, "You seemed to be watching over me. Why, oh why, did You let Grandfather get shot?" A single tear had escaped and trickled to her pillow. "For Jesus' sake, help him, and keep me safe."

When a smiling, neatly attired Duke Price appeared, she had swept him over with a glance, looked into his dark eyes, and decided he could be trusted. Besides, the station agent wouldn't have arranged for her to go with him if he wasn't all right. Being on her own wasn't easy, but Chantel was determined to make it. This was a wild land, no place for hesitancy.

Her first sight of tawny Brandon Morgan was not reassuring. The bold way he stopped them, the unspoken hostility between him and Duke, the arrogant way he took her over roused a fire of opposition. Yet he had said her grandfather sent him, although she would have preferred to remain with Duke.

The buckboard lived up to its name. Her body was as sore from jolting after they turned into the rutted road to the Triangle C as her spirit was from Brand's terrible accusations. How could anyone in his right mind suspect her of willfully seeking out a dying grandfather in order to inherit? She barely controlled a shudder.

Only once had he shown sympathy: It had flickered in his golden eyes when she let slip that she had no home but had died the next minute, leaving her aware that she had said something wrong.

Yet even her worry, anger, and discouragement could not dim the lure southwestern Montana Territory was weaving. She felt she could see almost forever. If

Brand hadn't been with her, she would have cried out over its beauty. Rolling lands and sagebrush, shining streams, distant hills, and white-topped mountains crowded one another for her attention. Wildflowers grew in abundance, until she longed to fill her hands and bury her face in them. If only Father were with her! Her face burned, her lips trembled. She must not think of him now.

She turned her attention to Brand, noticing how strong his hands were on the reins. They were as strong as the muscled arms that had cradled her when she fell. She bit her lip, vexed at herself. That moment had been one of security. It was all nonsense, she told herself. She despised this uncouth rancher, yet she could not deny the flare in her heart as she wrenched herself free. Unbidden came the memory of Arthur's fierce grasp, and how she had felt defiled. Brandon Morgan might be rough and unjust and accusing, but there had been no defilement in his touch. Only respect.

"We're almost there."

Chantel dropped her musing and leaned forward eagerly. "How beautiful!" She was aware of his quick glance and wished she'd kept silent. Yet how could she?

The Triangle C lay bathed in a yellow haze of sunlight. Never had she seen anything more peaceful. The long, low house hugged the ground. Its giant timbers, which surely must be trees split in half and smoothed, fit together snugly. Time had weathered them into a mellow monotone that fit into the surroundings. Trees she couldn't identify swayed in the slight breeze, dropping leaves to the already carpeted ground. A rude enclosure that must be what westerners called a corral housed a dozen horses. Men with bowed legs and colorful neckerchiefs moved among them, as well as among the countless red and white cattle dotting the fields past the house, adding spots of color to the land.

Yet nothing held Chantel's attention so much as the far-off mountains. They ascended from valley to sky in graduated steps, ending in a distant mass shimmering before her fascinated eyes. Even as she watched, great billowy clouds rose, caressing the mountaintops, boiling over into the blue sky, and dimming the day. In spite of the warm day, Chantel clutched her cloak closer. They were so like the storm clouds she had left behind! Only these were more frightening because of their visibility over the open land.

"Come." Brand had swung to the yard, stopped, and leaped down.

Chantel tore her attention from the sky, ignored the reaching hand, and climbed down, straightening her mussed traveling gown as she did so. A snicker from the corral drew her gaze like a magnet, and she tossed a haughty glance at the group of staring men. She recognized the cowboy who had told her about her grandfather, and his solemn blue eyes and shy smile told her he hadn't been the one who laughed. She nearly broke down at the kindness in his boyish face.

Meekly she followed Brand to the great door of the log house, seeing shining windows on each side and starched white curtains blowing in the afternoon breeze.

"Molly, this is Miss Evans, the old man's granddaughter. Miss Evans, Molly McLeod, the Triangle C housekeeper."

There was nothing in the pleasant face and welcoming blue eyes to show that Molly McLeod had not expected her, but Chantel suddenly knew she hadn't. She whirled on Brand. "You said Grandfather wanted me to come with you. He doesn't even know I'm here, does he? Why did you say that? Mr. Price would have brought me here." The long room stretching before her, with its huge fireplace, bouquets of wildflowers, and animal skins for rugs had reached out to her the moment she stepped inside.

"I didn't lie. If he'd known you were in Dillon, Charles would have sent me." Stern eyes dismissed her questions. "Molly, give Miss Evans a room. She'll want to get rid of some trail dust before she sees her grandfather."

That was exactly what Chantel would have wanted, but his high-handed way of ordering her about wasn't to be tolerated. She smiled at Molly and saw the corners of her mouth crinkle in answer. "I'm sure Grandfather has seen lots of trail dust, as you call it. Will you take me to him, please?"

"Of course, Miss Evans." Molly led the way to a closed door. "Remember, he's still pretty sick."

Chantel's rebellion died. "Then perhaps I should change while you tell him I'm here." Her eagerness to see her unknown grandfather hadn't taken into account what shock might do to him.

Molly's eyes were warm with approval. "Good. If you'll just follow me, Brand can break the good news to the old man." She led Chantel down a long hall into a small bedroom.

"Why does everyone call him that?" Chantel didn't mention that it sounded disrespectful to her Boston-trained ears.

Molly's eyes widened into twin lakes, reminding Chantel of Serena and her practical way of looking at things. "But that's what he's always been called. He wouldn't have it any other way." Her hands were busy pouring water into a basin. She disappeared and a few moments later came in with a kettle of steaming water to temper the cold water in the china basin. "Everyone in Montana knows and appreciates what he's done. Guess the only way we can show it is by callin' him that."

"Not everyone likes him, or he wouldn't have been shot."

Had the honest blue eyes grown evasive, or was it merely the shadow of tragedy so close? Molly patted Chantel's arm. "This is a big, wild country." Her fingers busied themselves with the fastenings on Chantel's dress. "Miss Evans, you'll find it frightening. Even the finest men make enemies."

"Please, call me Chantel."

The mobile mouth widened, showing strong white teeth. "I'd be proud to." She put the heavy traveling gown over her arm. "Wash up and I'll just run down and get a clean dress from your trunk." She was out into the long hall before Chantel could answer.

Chantel bathed her face, neck, and arms, glad to rid herself of the dust, then looked curiously around the room. There was no wallpaper here; the inside of the great logs had been whitewashed, and blankets in fantastic designs covered much of them. She supposed they must be Indian blankets.

The board floor had been waxed and shouldered its weight of animal skins as proudly as the living room floor had done. Starched curtains of snowy whiteness completed the charm of the room. How well everything blended. The fine skins and blankets and furniture must be handmade!

She had just taken down her hair and was brushing it when Molly returned. "Charles's favorite color is blue." She handed Chantel a simple blue cotton with fitted bodice and tiny lace edging on the collar and sleeves.

"It's warm." Chantel slipped into it.

"I just touched it up with an iron that was heatin' on the back of the cookstove." Molly helped her settle the folds, then said admiringly, "What beautiful hair you have."

Chantel flushed. Since her father died, there hadn't been many personal compliments. She deftly parted the wavy dark mane, braided it, and settled it firmly at the nape of her neck. Tiny tendrils escaped around her face to frame it.

"The boys out here'll be campin' on our doorstep," Molly told her with another smile. "How come those Boston lads ever let you escape?"

Every trace of color fled, leaving Chantel's face snowy.

"I didn't mean to pry," Molly apologized.

"It's all right." For a moment Chantel wanted to fling herself into Molly's aproned lap and cry, but the Evans pride stopped her. There must be no tears when she greeted her grandfather. She slowly followed the subdued Molly down the long hall, hoping Brand Morgan had gone. It would be unbearable to have his suspicions cloud her first meeting with her grandfather. Her heart sank as she saw him lounging in the open doorway of her grandfather's room.

"Here she is, Charles — your pretty granddaughter come all the way from Boston to visit."

She ignored what she thought was sarcasm and stepped inside, grudgingly grateful that Brand closed the door behind her, leaving her alone with the man in the low chair by the bed.

"Why, you're just like my father!"

Slow tears filled his watching eyes, and a smile crossed his thin face. "Chantel, you've come home!"

Straight as a speeding arrow she flew to him, only stopping at the last minute from throwing herself into his open arms. She dropped to her knees in front of him. Now that she was closer she saw that the resemblance between Charles, Sr., and Charles, Jr., was not physical. The man's gray hair and eyes betrayed age and hardship. Yet the feeling was there.

He took both hands in his own gnarled but strong ones. "How long can you stay?"

Her steady look never wavered. "Forever."

"Child, child, you're just like her!" The cry touched Chantel as nothing else could have done. "And you've come home."

A half-hour later, Molly's gentle tap and reminder that Charles must not overdo halted the flood of half-sentences, regrets, and joy of just being together. Chantel got up from her seat on a cushion on the floor, ecstatic. Her grandfather not only wanted her, he had learned to know her beloved friend Jesus during his stay in the dark valley so close to the river of death. She pressed a kiss on the furrowed brow where his hair parted and reluctantly went back to the big room.

Her happiness shattered at Brand's drawl. "I take it your meeting was successful." In her overwhelming gladness, she'd forgotten her escort and his suspicions. Rude reality clawed at her and she could only stare, then turn and walk to her room with as much dignity as she could muster, feeling his steel-hard eyes boring into her back.

Why did he hate her so? Even Lydia's animosity had been based on something tangible: the money and property. There had to be more reason for Firebrand Morgan, as she had learned he was often called, to dislike her so.

Her first few weeks on the Triangle C were so busy that she didn't have time to speculate much, but every time Brand came around — and that was often — the same carefully masked dislike made itself known. Charles and Molly, even the colorful Santa Fe, who was nearly recovered now, didn't seem to feel the barbs in what Brand said, but she was on edge every time he rode in.

By late July, Chantel felt as if she'd lived in Montana Territory forever. She'd never had many friends her own age, so she didn't miss the companionship of other girls. Her grandfather, Molly, and the hands were enough. To Rosy's delight, Chantel often asked him to ride with her. Charles had warned her against riding alone. There were too much country, wild animals, and wilder men for her to be safe. Molly had discarded Chantel's clothing as unsuitable for riding and produced an old but attractive deerskin suit, soft and supple as velvet.

"But I can't wear those," Chantel protested, holding up the short skirt, leggings, and chamois colored blouse. "I wouldn't feel ladylike!"

Charles's laugh rumbled in his chest. "Wear them. They're far more practical than any riding habit folks back east get up."

Reluctantly Chantel agreed to try them on. The image in the mirror startled her. If she let down her braid, she looked like a pale-skinned Indian girl. Her protest died. This was Montana Territory, she reminded herself. What was proper in Boston was ostentatious out here.

She hadn't known how much desire for

freedom had been inside her until Rosy pronounced her a real rider. She celebrated by pressing her heels into her Indian pony's sides and won the impromptu race back to the Triangle C.

It was on one of her rides that Chantel learned what had to be the real reason for Brand Morgan's feelings against her. She and Rosy had ridden to the mesa between the Triangle C and the Rocking M. The afternoon was peaceful, and she said, "This has to be the most beautiful place I've ever been."

Rosy looked from her tanned face to the valley below. "Yeah. Good thing Brand Morgan ain't the grudge-holdin' type." He must have seen her start of surprise, for he answered the question in her eyes while he sat at ease, one leg hooked over his saddle horn. Her friendliness had long since banished his shyness. "Before you came, everyone thought the old man'd leave the Triangle C to Brand. He's just like a son." He bit his lip. "Beggin' your pardon, ma'am."

"Why should my coming make any difference? Besides, Grandfather is getting better all the time," Chantel stated, irritation evident in her voice.

"The old man'll leave it to you, now. You're kin." Rosy's clear blue eyes widened in astonishment. "Doc says the boss still has to be careful."

Chantel scarcely heard him. A tiny pulse beat in her throat, and disgust nearly unseated her from her restless pony. So that was why he'd accused her of all those despicable things — because they were all true of himself! Brandon Morgan was just like the man in the Bible Jesus had called a fool, wanting more cattle and barns and lands to go with what he already had! No wonder he'd lashed out when he thought she might be a threat to him.

The valley below lost its sheen. The river turned sullen in Chantel's eyes, the mountains forbidding. Hot and cold by turns, even her attempts to pray silently were unsuccessful. She could taste fear in her mouth — metallic, sickening. Suppose that deadly ambition had disguised itself as a friend — just to get the Triangle C? She clutched the pommel for support as another thought beat into her brain: Suppose it had not been an unknown killer who shot Charles Evans and left him to die, but a rancher who sneaked on home and pretended shock when the old man was discovered?

Something inside Chantel shriveled. Impossible! Yet memory of the Colt revolver hanging low on Brand's hip haunted her. She no longer felt safe and welcome here, but more frightened than she'd ever been before. God, was there no place free of greed and hatred?

"Ma'am, are you all right?"

Rosy's worried face swam before her eyes. She shook herself and produced a smile. "Fine. A little dizzy. Maybe it's too warm." She let him help her from the saddle, heard the clink of spurs as he fetched the canteen, and let the cool water slide down her parched throat. Reason took over. If Brand had planned such a monstrous thing, he could have carried it out long before now. The valley resumed its friendly appearance, and she sighed with relief.

Yet a few weeks later, when she came in from riding and found the doctor there, her heart leaped to her throat. "What is it?" she asked Molly, who was white-faced and still.

"The old man had some kind of spell. I sent for Doc. He's in there now." Her fingers bit into Chantel's arm as she impulsively took a step forward. "Leave them be."

Would Doc never finish? Chantel wanted to scream. Instead she stood fixed to the spot, even when Brand Morgan strode through the great front door and said harshly, "What's wrong?"

"Old man's sick." Molly moistened her lips with her tongue. "Doc's with him."

How had Brand learned something was wrong so quickly? Chantel forgot her question as Doc came out and closed the door.

"What's the trouble?" There was no denying the concern in Brand's question.

"His ticker's acting up."

Chantel couldn't speak.

Brand roared, "Come on, Doc, the old man's heart's stronger than Eagle Peak!"

Doc shook his head. "Not anymore. Being shot was a strain." He averted his gaze after one look at Chantel. "Barring any sudden shock, he'll live through the winter." He blew his nose loudly.

"But — you must do something for him!" Chantel found her voice and protested.

"When the good Lord says time's up, it's up. Nothing I can do." He banged out the door, leaving havoc in the room.

"The good Lord!" Brand's lips curled back in a snarl. "Fine lot of good —"

"Stop!" Chantel covered her ears. "I won't listen to your blasphemies. My grandfather won't, either." Reeling with shock, she still had spirit enough to speak for her Lord. "We can't fight God. If we did, we wouldn't win." She swallowed and forced herself to look straight into Brand's angry face. "We won't be bothering Grandfather with useless threats against God." She slipped inside the sickroom and closed the door behind her, aware of total stillness in the big living room.

"Come here, child."

The few steps to the bed lengthened to miles as she slowly paced them off. "You know?"

"Yes." The lined face softened. "My only regret's not having had you here sooner. I've learned to know my Lord, and now I'm looking forward to seeing Him and your father."

Blinding tears came in sheets, yet with them came cleansing. "I'm going to miss you so much." She lifted her face steadfastly. "But we're going to make every day we have count." A butterfly smile hovered across her face. "I won't go riding or —"

"Of course you will!" His keen look scorched her. "You're going to ride and take it all in, then come back and tell me what you've seen." He grimaced. "Don't s'pose Doc'll let me get out."

Chantel did as he asked. Every evening

was spent with him, sharing, often praying together. As Charles prepared to forsake his earthly kingdom for a distant heavenly land, Chantel grew closer to him than anyone she'd ever known, except her father. Word got around and visitors came in droves, but always the evenings belonged to just the two of them. Once Chantel was surprised to hear him ask, "You once told me you'd stay forever. Do you still feel that way?" All she could do was nod, but it satisfied him. "Then I've done right."

Molly McLeod came and went. Santa Fe saw to the business of the ranch. When reports of missing cattle came in, no one told Charles. In spite of Doc's predictions, the old man was failing. Chantel refused to admit it, but deep inside she knew the falling leaves would in all probability cover her grandfather's grave. She gave no thought to afterwards. It was enough learning to accept her loss and knowing Charles would be in her Lord's hands.

September stole by in a blaze of yellow and gold. October first was so gorgeous that Charles insisted Chantel ride. One look at his emaciated face stilled her protest and she obediently climbed into her riding outfit. By the time she got to the corral, all the hands were out in the hills.

What should she do? She'd been told never to ride alone, but now that she was a proficient horsewoman, there would be no danger. She wouldn't stay long, anyway. She'd dawdled, and darkness fell early this time of year.

"Come on, Chinook." She mounted and turned toward her favorite spot, the one overlooking the river. The big flat rock on top was warm with the sun, enticing. Dropping her reins, she stretched out. It was so good just to lie still! In spite of acceptance, her impending loss had kept her awake nights. She'd close her eyes and rest.

Hours later a horrid scream filled the air. Chantel sat bolt upright, aware of how cold she was and how dark it had grown. "Chinook?" A nervous whinny answered, then was drowned by another shrill scream. The reins she'd fumbled to find in the darkness were pulled from her hands by the terrified horse, who reared and bolted.

Chantel scrambled to her feet. "Chinook! Come back!" Her voice floated into the valley, echoing from a distant cliff. She was alone on the bluff with some creature in the darkness that could see her. Why hadn't she listened when she'd been told never to ride alone?

She reached inside her blouse for the small gun Grandfather had insisted she learn to use and carry. How much good would it do against the unseen menace that could be stalking her right now? Perspiration sprang to her forehead and turned cold in the chill fall air. She faltered. Should she try and follow the trail in the darkness or stay where she was?

Another scream, even closer, decided her. With a cry to God for help, she turned in the direction Chinook had taken and fled down the winding trail, little heeding the stickery brush reaching out to tear her leggings and skirt. Once a low branch of a tree whipped her across the face, and she slowed. She must not be knocked out.

Her nightmare descent finally ended, and she stopped at the bottom, panting. Was that the lights of the Triangle C twinkling in the distance?

A little cry of gladness burst from her. It would take time, but all she had to do was keep her eye firmly fixed on the light. She started forward, keenly aware of the tiny rocks embedded in her bleeding hands when she had fallen. Ignoring their smarting, she hurried as fast as she could, trying to avoid sage brush that perfumed the night but slowed her progress.

The sudden drumming of hooves brought her new terror. Every tale of wild men she had heard lent speed to her feet, but the restless pursuit went on. Who was after her? Why didn't he speak? Her energy was nearly gone, and still the rider came. Creaking leather gave way to a "Whoa!" She turned her head. Faint starlight showed a bulky figure leaping from the saddle of a snorting horse. She stumbled, fell, and was pounced on by someone with hands like bands of iron.

"Who —" she gasped.

"You crazy, inconsiderate fool!"

Only one person in Montana Territory would dare speak so to Charles Evans's granddaughter. *"You!"*

Brand Morgan's features shone in the faint light. "Don't you know what you've done?"

She tried to wrench free, but his hands sank deeper into her arms. "I fell asleep. Chinook ran away. I couldn't help it." Her teeth rattled as he shook her.

"You've succeeded in killing the old man!"

This time she jerked free in spite of his cruel grip. *"What are you saying?"*

"Haven't you been told not to go off alone? Molly covered for you until supper.

Then a masked rider came in and threw a rock with a paper wrapped around it in the front window. There was no keeping it from Charles."

Chantel marveled that words could get through her constricted throat. "What did it say?"

"That you were being held for ransom." With a mighty scoop, he picked her up, threw her on the big horse, then climbed up behind her. She could see his set, gleaming face above her. "The old man kicked Molly out of his room and got dressed. He made it to the front yard."

"He's dead?" She clutched the horse's mane and swayed.

"Yes. That God you both pray to must have shut down business. Charles lived exactly five minutes after he fell." The grim, relentless words fell from his lips like a death knell. "Just long enough to tell Molly and Santa Fe to take care of his beloved granddaughter." He jerked the reins viciously, and called, "Go on, Dark Star. We must get this precious piece of womanhood to her newly inherited ranch."

8

If Chantel had ever doubted her grandfather's importance to Montana Territory,
the number of people who came for the
simple graveside service would have convinced her. There were over a hundred
present and countless messages from those
who couldn't come. She read them over,
fiercely rejoicing in the place he had won in
the hearts of friends and neighbors. The service itself was short, as Charles Evans had
left instructions for it to be, but filled with
the hope of one who had accepted a resur-
rected Lord and looked forward.

Then it was over. The lawyer who'd
drawn up Charles's will took Chantel
aside. "No use delaying reading the will."
His eyes looked resigned. "If it's all right
with you, we'll just go ahead and I can get
back to town."

Chantel nodded mutely, uncaring. What
had to be done might as well be faced. Her

grandfather's body lay in a fresh mound under a cottonwood tree next to the faded marker of his wife. Yet his spirit seemed close.

When Chantel, Molly, Santa Fe, and Brand Morgan gathered in the living room, the lawyer cleared his throat and looked around. "Duke Price needs to be here, too."

Chantel saw Brand's mouth twist. Duke had made good his promise to visit the Triangle C several times, but any time Brand was present, there had been a hidden current flowing with unasked questions. Chantel fingered her white dress; her grandfather had asked her not to wear mourning. Why was Duke Price being called?

When Santa Fe came back with the dark cowboy, who seemed a bit unfamiliar in what Molly called "city clothes," the lawyer cleared his throat again. "You all know why you're here: to hear Charles Evans's will." He unfolded a paper and began to read, then stopped. "No need to go through all the 'whyfors' and 'whereases.' It's plain and simple. Molly's to be allowed to stay at the Triangle C as long as she lives. Santa Fe's to remain on as foreman as long as he wants to stay. The stretch of land separating the Triangle C and the Rocking M down by the Bannock Creek crossing is to go to Brand. Everything else is to belong to Miss Chantel Evans, as long as she lives here on the Triangle C." He cleared his throat again and bent a stern gaze on Chantel. "Should you decide to go back east, all you have inherited — except for a few hundred dollars — will be given to Brandon Morgan."

His papers shuffled noisily in the silent room. "There are two more provisions. In the event you should die without a child, everything reverts to Brand." He looked at Chantel steadily.

"I refuse to accept such terms!" Brand was on his feet, face dark with fury.

"Sit down," the lawyer ordered. "I intend to see Charles Evans's will is carried out to the letter of the law."

"I won't sit down, and I won't stand for such a will." The arrogant toss of his head accented his words. "Are you all so dumb you don't see where it puts me?" Venom shone in the look he directed at Chantel. "She goes out and pulls some fool stunt and gets herself killed. What happens? I inherit and everyone in Montana Territory secretly believes I planned it to get the Triangle C!"

His ringing denunciation filled Chantel with a sneaking admiration, but she hastily squashed it. Wasn't this the best way of all to declare innocence in the event that what he predicted came to pass?

"I hardly think we need spend any more time with your dramatics," the lawyer said dryly. "The second provision was added just a few weeks ago." The high forehead wrinkled. "It's more of a personal note than anything else." He adjusted his spectacles and read: "To Duke Price I leave my apologies. Any embarrassment or trouble he has suffered on my account is highly regretted."

Chantel saw a flash in Duke's eyes that was quickly covered — so quickly that she wondered if she could have been mistaken.

Brand's catlike eyes narrowed. "Just what's that supposed to mean?" He took one step closer to the lawyer.

"Who knows?" The lawyer placed the papers in his pocket and shrugged, obviously glad to be free of obligation. He turned his back on Brand to face Chantel. "Well, Miss Evans?"

Molly McLeod burst out, "Land sakes, give the child a chance to think! She'll be needin' time to take in all that's happened without you gawkin' men around. Out."

"Just as you say, Molly. We peons mustn't bother the new owner of the Triangle C." Brand strode through the door without looking back. Santa Fe mumbled something and followed, then the lawyer. As Molly bustled toward the kitchen, a curious incident that didn't register with Chantel at the time but haunted her later took place. Duke stood before her, hat in hand. "I'm sorry, Miss Evans. He was a grand old man." He stepped away, hesitated, then softly said, "Be very careful." The next instant he was gone.

"Chantel, you need to eat a bite." Molly reappeared in the doorway, tying an enveloping apron over her Sunday dress.

It was easier to eat than to protest. But when twilight fell, that time of day she'd loved so, she slipped into the dusk and wandered back to the giant cottonwood whose roots lovingly cradled a fresh grave. It was the first time since Brand packed her home that she'd been alone. Molly had even insisted on setting up a cot in her room and sleeping there. It was almost a relief to escape the loving care. She must think. As long as her grandfather had been alive, the Triangle C was home. Could it still be, without his presence?

She thought of the house in Boston that

was legally hers but that she had left to save scandal. "I won't go back." A night bird's cry mingled with the far-off howl of a wolf. They no longer bothered her; they were part of the land.

Her head drooped, but no tears fell. She couldn't wish her grandfather back. He had made what he felt was the best provision for her. No wonder he'd asked how she felt about Montana Territory. By making sure the Triangle C was hers, he'd given her a home. If she chose to turn her back on it, it would belong to a man who loved it.

"I spoke to the lawyer." Brand's harsh voice sliced the gloom.

Chantel started. "About what?"

He towered over her and she struggled to her feet, unwilling to be at such a disadvantage.

"He's agreed you can sell out to me. Go back to Boston where you belong. You needn't think I'll claim jump the Triangle C. I'll buy it at a fair price and pay you before you leave."

"I'm not leaving."

"Why not? You got what you came for, didn't you? The ranch?" His mocking voice infuriated her to speechlessness. "I have to admit, you even got fond of the old

147

man. But he's gone. This is no place for a girl. Go spend the money and remember us once in awhile."

Chantel's reply was sheer mastery of words over emotion. "You were right, Mr. Morgan. I got what I came for. I told you that first day I wanted a home. I found one — and I'm keeping it."

"Oh?" Total disbelief turned the single syllable into contempt. "Just how do you aim to do that?"

"Why," she gathered her scattered senses, "Molly and Santa Fe and I will run the ranch as we did while Grandfather was sick."

"You run the Triangle C?" The heavens echoed his laughter. "You don't think the boys will stand for a woman boss?"

Chantel stepped around him and started back to the house. "I don't see why not." Chin high, eyes fixed on the lamp in the window, she walked straight ahead.

"Lady, you do have a lot to learn."

She spun toward the sound of his voice. "I never said I didn't. I know I wasn't born here and raised on the Triangle C. I wish I had been." She tried in vain to see his expression. "But God will help me do what I must, and running the Triangle C is part of it." He didn't reply, and she retreated, her vision clouded and her heart pounding. She'd made her own little declaration of independence because he'd goaded her into it. Now she was glad. This was her home. Other eastern girls had learned how to be pioneers when there were far worse things to fight than a neighboring rancher. She would too.

A nagging suspicion that Brand might be right prodded her. What was the best way to approach her problems? "Molly," she called as she raced into the house, "tell Santa Fe I want to see every cowboy who works for the Triangle C in the yard tomorrow morning at six o'clock sharp."

The lamp shone brightly on Molly's astonished face.

"Good night, Molly. See you in the morning." She flashed down the hall before her housekeeper could answer, glad she'd finally convinced Molly to move the cot from its temporary home. She needed this night to prepare.

Long after the last snatch of laughter floated up from the bunkhouse and the last steer's shuffling feet stilled for the night, Chantel lay sleepless. The magnitude of what lay ahead appalled her. It was easy to tell Brand Morgan what she would do, but accomplishing it was going to be far more difficult. Still, hadn't her Lord promised to walk beside her, to protect and comfort her? With a great sigh of relief, she turned on her side and slept.

It was good she had prepared herself. Even Rosy stood with averted face when she stepped on the porch the next morning, clutching a heavy coat around her shoulders against the early air. "I suppose you all know why I've called you together." She inhaled sharply. "By now you've heard I'm the new owner of the Triangle C. I've heard things about you, too. I've heard that you won't work for me because I'm a woman."

She drew herself to full height, meeting the frank gazes of her riders. "I'm twenty one today — a woman. I don't pretend to know about cattle ranching, but I intend to learn." Could they hear the beating of her heart through her coat? "Will you give me a chance?"

There wasn't a sound until a voice from the back said, "Aw, I ain't ridin' for no woman. Especially an easterner." A rumble of assent swept through the ranks of men, and her heart fell. She had appealed to them and failed.

"Hold on now, boys." Santa Fe lifted his sombrero, smoothed back sandy hair, and grinned. "The little lady's called us here and laid her cards out open. She ain't sayin' she knows what she don't. All she's askin' for is a chance. She's the old man's granddaughter. Don't she deserve that?"

Another rumble greeted his words, and Chantel held her breath.

"You're just stickin' because you're sweet on Molly," someone called. A roar of laughter broke out.

Santa Fe's face reddened, but he grinned again. "Sure am." He ducked a glance at the now-empty kitchen window where Molly's face had been before. His smile faded. "Old man's always been good about keepin' us on durin' the winter, not like a lot of the ranchers that let the boys go. I for one ain't hankerin' to light out and try and get a job now."

"What're we supposed to tell the other guys if we stay and work for a tenderfoot girl?"

"Tell them she may not be a rancher but she's prettier than any of their bosses," Santa Fe flashed back. "Howsomever, any of you boys who want your time, speak up right now."

The crowd was quiet until the discontented cowhand from the back came forward, shoving his buddies aside. "Just one little thing. Who's going to be givin' the orders?"

If Chantel hadn't been so relieved, she'd have smiled at the cowboy's little-boy truculence. "Santa Fe is your foreman, just as he's always been. Any order I have will be discussed with him. He knows this business, this country. I don't. At least not yet."

The rumble gave way to approval. "Fair enough," Rosy hollered. "Miss Chantel's got my time."

She beamed at him, delighted at his championship.

"Mine, too."

"And mine."

One by one they doffed their hats.

Chantel smiled and said huskily, "Thank you. Santa Fe will tell you anything else you need to know."

"Miss boss, how about a raise?" There was sheer deviltry in the question.

Chantel started to speak. Maybe it would be a good idea. She caught Santa Fe's sidelong glance and almost imperceptible shake of his head. "Sorry, boys. Like I said, Santa Fe's in charge." As she stepped back inside the house, she caught a low comment: "She ain't gonna be a pushover, in spite of that pretty face."

"You did just fine, honey." Molly beamed her satisfaction. "Never let the boys think they got the best of you, or they'll rag you unmercifully."

In the following days Chantel discovered what Molly meant. She made the mistake of dressing one of the boys' arms after a nasty spill and found her ranch hands using every excuse to have her take care of their cuts and bruises, too! She could no longer use Rosy as escort. The other boys complained it wasn't fair and wanted to take turns riding with her.

Exasperated by their antics, Chantel finally told Santa Fe to threaten to fire the whole lot of them if they didn't settle down. This dampened their ardor, and she got some peace. Yet through it all she had begun to love her "boys," as she classified them, although most were older than she. Mischievous as they were, they were also hardworking, and as she learned, loyal. She didn't realize how loyal until mid-November, when work on the ranch was at its lightest. Harness mending and the shoeing of stock was nearly done. Riding the frozen fields to look for winterbound cattle hadn't started yet.

"Too much free time," Santa Fe fumed. "And that —" he swallowed what Chantel knew must be a curse — "that Chantel saloon's filled every night."

"With our boys?" Chantel was horrified.

"Yup. They're givin' their devils a run."

"Can't it be shut down?" Color filled Chantel's face. "I'll talk to Duke Price about it."

He was strangely adamant. "They aren't hurting anything. Just celebrating a little free time." Nothing she could say convinced him differently, which left her surprised and hurt. Santa Fe was always a perfect gentleman, at least around her, so why did he persist in allowing and encouraging that den of iniquity at the edge of her land?

One Sunday afternoon she restlessly prowled the ranch house. It had been months since she'd been to church. She missed it, but it was too far to ride into Dillon, where the nearest preacher held services. In desperation she dropped to the low stool in front of the spinet that had been hauled in by wagon for the first Chantel. Her fingers drifted into half-forgotten melodies. Daylight disappeared and evening shadows deepened, and still she played. She and Molly sometimes read their Bibles together, but she missed services.

It was nearly dark in the room except for the now-dying fire when she grew aware of a presence in the room. "Molly?"

"No." The masculine voice came from the overstuffed chair by the fireplace.

"Why, Mr. Morgan!" It had been weeks since he'd visited the Triangle C. "Why didn't you announce yourself? Where's Molly?"

"In the kitchen. I told her not to disturb you, that I'd just drop down and listen."

Uncomfortable in the dim light, Chantel took a splinter from the fire and lit the big kerosene lamp, driving back the shadows with its brightness. "Did you want anything special?" She noticed he was spruced up. Although he wore an open-necked shirt and gay kerchief, they looked new. The ever-present gun belt with its hanging burden repelled her. "Must you wear that all the time?"

"It's a good thing I was wearing it last week."

"What do you mean?"

"If I hadn't, your friend Rosy wouldn't be around to tell about it." His level look impaled her like a butterfly on a pin. "Didn't you see the way he looked?"

"I noticed he was scratched and bruised." Chantel faltered, hating the apol-

155

ogetic note in her voice. Why did this man always bring out the worst in her, or make her feel guilty of some unnamed crime? "He said his horse threw him."

"Funny, I could have sworn I picked him up off the floor of the Chantel saloon after the owner beat him up for arguing when he called this ranch the Sunday school C. I got in at the tail end of things, just in time to stop Rosy from getting shot."

"I didn't know." Her knees buckled, depositing Chantel in a chair.

"No, you wouldn't. You think all it takes is making a pretty speech and smiling and getting the boys to like you, and the ranch is run. But it takes men to fight your battles. Rosy could've been killed."

"Did you shoot the saloon owner?" Chantel couldn't hold back her horrified question, torn between fear and desire to hear it wasn't true.

"Winged him."

"How can you just sit there and talk about shooting a man?" His laconic statement roused every righteous feeling she had.

"Would you rather I'd have let Rosy die?"

She sank back, unable to speak.

"Miss Boss, they call you. Well, Miss

Boss, you'd better hightail it out of here and let someone handle the Triangle C who's a whole lot better at it than you'll ever be."

"Sir, you are insulting!" The unprovoked attack brought color to Chantel's parchment-like face.

"And you are ruining the Triangle C. Don't you think the whole country's laughing at your lovesick cowhands who'll fight at the drop of a hat if anyone dares criticize you?"

"At least you don't seem to have that malady." Caution was thrown aside as she sprang from her chair, hot tears crowding her eyelids.

He looked her over the way she fancied he'd look at a prize steer he was considering buying. "It might not be so bad at that." He lazily got to his feet, his eyes glowing golden. "Since you won't go away and the Triangle C's going downhill fast, I might be persuaded to help you out."

"I can't imagine any way you could ever help me." Yet her heart raced as his eyes narrowed.

"I could marry you."

A cannonball at her feet couldn't have rocked Chantel more. She could feel fury rise from her toes, warring against every gentle Christian instinct she'd tried to develop. Powerless to move or speak, she saw him advance, a slight smile on his lips. The next moment his strong arms closed around her and his lips found hers, not in the wild, seeking demand she would have expected from his untamed nature, but gently, almost reverently.

Reverent! The thought tore her free from his spell. "You — you —"

"I apologize, Miss Evans. I had no right to do that — yet." But there was no apology in the gold eyes, just a look that sent Chantel's gaze to her feet as he crossed the room. Every indictment she longed to cast, every accusation about his despicable action, rose to confront her too late. A wild "Yahoo" and a rush of horse's flying hooves thrust scarlet into her face.

"How could I have let him?" she whispered brokenly. "Why didn't I fight, pull free? He's everything unholy. He laughs at God. He carries a gun and uses it. Yet I allowed him to —" she buried her face in her hands, denying the feelings churning inside her as she remembered his touch. From the swirling mists of memory came Serena's voice that long-ago day on the train. "Some Montana cowboy will be building a cabin." Then, "Wild cowboys met truehearted girls, settled down, became Christian examples."

"Impossible!" She faced the window, staring into the darkness. "He could never accept Jesus."

Why did her heart sink at the statement? Why should she care? Yet she did care. It was suddenly the most important thing in her world for Brandon Morgan to meet and know and love her Lord. She couldn't face her new knowledge, and was glad when Molly came in.

"Where's Brand? Thought he'd like a bite to eat before he left."

Chantel managed a little laugh. "He's always in a hurry." She abandoned her pose. "Molly, what's he really like?"

"He's the fairest man in western Montana Territory, now your grandfather's gone. And maybe the most ruthless. He rides our wild land with iron-shod boots, and it's men like him that are settlin' the west."

Chantel's heart sank even lower. "Could a man like that ever — ever know the Lord?"

"Your grandfather did."

"But he was never as wild as Mr. Morgan!"

"The way I hear tell it, Brand doesn't

measure up at all to what Charles Evans had to be to settle out here."

Chantel's dark head drooped. She didn't want to see Molly's face when she answered the question Chantel burned to ask. "Has Mr. Morgan ever been involved with women?" A hot blush rose to her hairline. "I mean the wrong kind of women."

Molly said quickly, "Not the wrong kind or any other kind." She laughed. "Not because the gals wouldn't have liked it that way. I remember about five years ago there was a story goin' the rounds about a filly he'd been polite to up in Helena durin' a cattle-selling meeting. She ups and writes she's comin' down to visit. According to Duke, she was aiming to get hitched, and any man who treated her decent was fair game.

"Anyway, Brand doesn't want to hurt her feelings, so he gets Duke to write and tell her he's been sick. Next comes a letter saying she's about to hotfoot it down here and nurse him! So the ornery devil puts Duke up to writing he's sorry, but Brand's died." She stopped for breath, enjoyment of the story spreading across her face.

"That's terrible!"

"That ain't all. Somehow the gal gets hold of Charles's name and learns he's a good friend of Duke and Brand. She sends a long letter expressing her sympathy over the death of such a fine young man and money so's Charles can put flowers on Brand's grave for her!"

Chantel couldn't help joining in Molly's contagious laughter. "I think it's perfectly awful."

"Not so awful as when Brand had to go back to Helena. He spent the whole time ducking around corners to keep out of her way, so she'd not find out what he and Duke had done." Molly folded her hands. "Since then he's never been known to be overly polite to girls and women. I'd hoped after you came that —"

"Really," Chantel felt the blood rush to her head, "you don't honestly think Brandon Morgan and I could," she stumbled over the word *care,* "could be friends! Not after all he accused me of doing."

"He doesn't believe what he's accusing you of," Molly told her. "I think he's just not sure why you upset him all the time, and this's his way of covering up." She rubbed her forehead. "Charles felt the same way."

"Grandfather!" Chantel stared open-mouthed. "When did you ever discuss me in relation to Mr. Morgan?"

161

"It wasn't my idea, so don't get bothered." Molly turned the lamp wick down. "I just know a few days before he died, his face got all wistful and he said, 'Molly, if Chantel and Brand ever got together, it'd be just grand for them both. He'd protect her, and she'd soften him.'" Molly's voice lowered into an Irish brogue. "Shure, an' if the Good Lord sent you out here for that, it'd be a fine thing."

Chantel slowly followed the dimming lamp as Molly led the way down the hall, her heart beating until she felt she would suffocate. Could there be any remote possibility that Molly and her grandfather were right? Warring forces rose to attack the preposterous idea. They were from different worlds. Far more separated them than east and west. Never again would she allow herself to consider being yoked with an unbeliever, and Brand Morgan gloried in being just that.

9

Shortly after Charles Evans died and Chantel turned twenty-one she wrote a long letter to Mr. Barker. She glossed over her reasons for leaving Boston and merely stated the bare facts: She had come west to visit her grandfather; he had died after making a will leaving her the Triangle C, and she planned to stay. She closed by requesting him to let her know if her inheritance had been settled. Then she promptly forgot it in the never-ending round of duties. Santa Fe had a habit of dropping in with problems to be discussed. Chantel had started taking cooking lessons from Molly, determined to master the light bread, pies, and rich stews Molly served. Only on Sundays did she rest.

This sunup-to-sundown existence was paying off. The weak, trembling girl who'd come to the ranch burst from her cocoon, but she was no butterfly. It was true that her beauty had deepened, but her spirit was spreading its wings even more. The time she spent alone with her Lord was refining her soul. Even when she slipped and allowed anger with Brand or the Chantel saloon owner to overcome her, always in the back of her mind was the gentle way her Master would have responded. It showed in her face, and while her cowboys didn't understand, they could feel it.

Duke Price was bold enough to comment, "Why aren't you like other gals, Chantel?" They had long been on a first-name basis. "You're different."

"I know." Her rueful smile was at herself, not him. "But I'm learning. See?" She held out a slim hand, no longer white and useless. There was a blister on the palm. The back was still tanned from summer and a bit scratched.

"I didn't mean that." Duke's eyes were dark as her own. She could see double reflections of herself in them as he watched her. "It's something else, an almost spiritual thing." He laughed as if ashamed to be caught discussing such things.

Chantel caught her breath. Did she dare seize the opening to say a word for her Lord? She let her lashes hide her eyes. "If I'm different, maybe it's because you haven't known a lot of Christian girls." Her voice was gentle, but Duke winced.

"You're right there. If they're Christians, they aren't saying so." His intent gaze never left her face. "You really think it makes that much difference?" He pointed out the window to the snowcovered land glistening in the sun. "When I'm out there, I know it didn't just happen. Somebody had to be in charge." His laugh was a bit strained, and Chantel didn't miss the look in his eyes. "Maybe I'm a Christian and don't even know it!"

"No, Duke, No!"

He turned from staring through the window. "I'm not such a bad guy." A brooding look settled over his dark face. "I'm not everything you've probably heard I am."

Chantel searched for words to make him understand. Beneath her warm wool dress, her heart beat faster. Could she make him understand? "It isn't being what we think is good or bad. It isn't even believing there's a God." She caught his bewildered look. "No one can be a Christian without seeing he or she's a sinner and asking God to forgive. That's why Jesus came and died on the cross, to save us. He paid the penalty of our sins. What we have to do is believe and accept that as a free gift."

It wasn't the last time they discussed it. Duke became her companion during the winter months, and many times they talked of what being a Christian meant. Once he said, "If I got to be a Christian and asked you to think about me as a husband, would it be all right?"

Chantel hesitated. What she said was vitally important. A silent prayer for guidance winged upwards. "Duke, you must never accept the Lord for the sake of another person." Her throat ached. "I hope and pray you do, but it can't be for me but for yourself — and Him." The little pool of silence between them widened to a lake. "Besides —" her voice failed her.

"Besides   " his big hand covered hers and misery shone in his dark eyes. "You only like me as a pard, not a future husband." He gripped her hand, then released it and grinned. "I'm glad for that, anyway!"

What a paradox he was! Chantel tremulously smiled back. It would be easy to love him. He was dark, courteous, respectful. Why, in all the time she'd known him, this was the first time he'd ever spoken of feelings or touched her, except to help her dismount when they were riding. And he was so close to the kingdom of God! For a split second she longed to care about him, yet deep inside was the knowledge that warm friendship could never be enough. She had been chastened over allowing the desire for security to involve her with Arthur Masters. Not again. If God intended her to marry one day, she would have to know it with all her heart.

Why should the memory of a single kiss bring flaming color to her face? There must be something wrong with her to fancy anything could ever be between her and a wild rancher with tawny hair and eyes. He was too like the tawny mountain lions that preyed on stock to be tamed.

"Does Brand get over much?"

Good heavens, could Duke read her mind? Her chest heaved, but she managed to say, "Not recently. He's probably very busy." On impulse she added, "Didn't you used to be partners?"

"Yes."

The word hung in the air. After the clock ticked off a full minute, Chantel realized Duke wasn't going to elaborate. She tossed a stick of wood on the already surging fire and exclaimed, "Although it's beautiful now, I can hardly wait for spring."

She sensed Duke's relief as he agreed, "It's something to see. Every creek and

167

river swells, and the whole world turns green. Is Santa Fe planning for a spring roundup?"

"Not for shipping. He says we'd be better off fattening them up on summer grass and selling in the fall."

Duke's face darkened. "More chance of losing to rustlers that way." He abruptly dropped the subject. "Did you ever find out who sent that ransom note the day the old man died?"

"No." She couldn't meet his probing look and turned away to watch the fire. A months-old memory jogged her. "The day of the funeral, why did you tell me to be careful?"

He stood with the liquid motion that she'd come to associate with him. "A person can't be too careful in this country. If someone threatened once, he might again." His voice was just a shade too casual, and Chantel eyed him carefully. "Not all the varmints around here travel on four feet," he added.

Chantel had the feeling she was being warned again but couldn't quite figure it out. "Things have been peaceful enough this winter." She couldn't resist adding, "Except for the problems caused by the saloon."

Duke didn't respond to her implied question, just smiled. "Good-bye, Chantel, I'll see you soon." He left while the troubled girl stayed by the roaring fire, trying to understand.

One good thing that came with winter was the deepening love between Molly and Chantel and the lowering of Molly's resistance to Santa Fe's devotion. The same day Chantel awoke to a world strangely denuded of snow, Molly blushingly announced, "Soon's spring roundup for countin' cows is over, Santa Fe and I are gettin' married. It's all right, isn't it? We'll still be livin' here."

"It's fine." Chantel stared at them both. "But when did you decide?" She laughed. "How'd you get her to agree, Santa Fe?"

Santa Fe's dry retort couldn't hide his happiness. "The Chinook done it. The snow wasn't the only thing that melted 'round here."

Chantel ran to the front door and threw it wide. "Serena Farley told me about the Chinook." She gasped. Where snow had stretched unendingly, now brown ground reigned, except for occasional patches of white melting around the edges. "I never knew it'd be like this." Suddenly she wanted to sing. "I have to ride. I just have to ride!"

"Breakfast first, young lady," Molly ordered with the loving tyranny she affected. "Then Santa Fe can take you to see the rivers and streams."

An hour later Chantel reined in Chinook, aptly named for his fleetness, and nearly fell from her saddle. Her shocked, "That's Bannock Creek?" echoed across the mighty expanse of muddy water before her.

"Sure is." If Santa Fe's chuckle was any indication, he was enjoying her reaction. "Quite a piece of water, ain't it?"

That was sheer understatement. The usually sparkling stream had grown turgid and roiling, spilling over its banks to gnaw at the land on both sides.

"Water comes down from the mountains," Santa Fe explained as a chunk of tree with waving branches sailed past. "If there's any kind of jam, it builds up and tears it out like an avalanche. Time's been when I've seen a wall of water twenty feet high roaring down a draw." He turned and pointed to the distant snowy peaks. "Soon all but the topmost snow'll be melting. Then spring will be here."

A strangely subdued Chantel rode home later, mud spattered and tired. The fascination of the flooded creek had held her motionless. Never had she been faced with such a sight, and something inside her cried out, an exultant thrill over the majesty of her Creator who could set in motion such forces, yet love His people enough to provide a way of forgiveness.

"How much else is there to learn about this country?" she demanded of Molly as they worked together preparing supper. "Just when I think I know this country, it turns around and does something unexpected."

"That's the way to live in Montana Territory." Molly's hands stopped punching down dough. "It's when you least expect it that somethin' new comes along. I remember the day they brought my husband home." Pain laced her forehead, making her look old for a moment. "I'd been baking his favorite apple pies, humming and happy. Then they came and told me he'd been killed."

"How could you stand it?"

"At first I didn't think I could," Molly said simply. "Then I got to remembering all the good years we'd been given and thanked the Lord for what I'd had, instead of regretting what I'd lost."

Chantel's eyes were wet. "Now you're going to be happy again."

"In a different way." Molly smiled, and the dough was lifted and punched down again. "Santa Fe knows he'll never take my first husband's place, but he doesn't want to. He's just asking for a place of his own." She expertly separated the dough and began patting it into little mounds. "I fought it off a long time. After he got shot last summer, I knew what life'd be without him. If he'd asked me anytime after that, I'd have agreed."

"You knew and didn't tell him? Why?" Chantel asked.

"A man likes to do the courting. Oh, they're flattered and all that if a woman follows them, but they like to feel they've ridden at the head of the herd. So I waited till Santa Fe spoke again."

"You're a fraud," Chantel accused through her laughter. Then she sobered. "Molly." She hesitated, uncertain of how to go on without trespassing. "You're a Christian. Will you be happy with Santa Fe?"

"Law, child," Molly's eyebrows rose in peaks. "Santa Fe may seem rough, but down inside he's a real Christian. Accepted the Lord back when he was just a splinter. He don't go around spouting what he believes, but it's there. It's hard for him to show how

172

he feels, although he was telling Brand Morgan the other day that if he ever wanted to be real happy he'd better quit making war on God and get to asking His pardon."

"He said that to Brand?"

"I was there. Brand had ridden in just for a minute." Molly's keen gaze concentrated on her biscuits after a lightning-swift glance at Chantel. "You were riding with Duke. Brand said something about wondering if the rustlers could be caught and this range made a better place for decent folk. He looked so miserable when he added, 'The old man's better off out of it.' I like to have cried. Then Santa Fe hitched up his britches and said his say."

Chantel felt her lungs would burst from holding her breath. "What did Brand say?"

A scowl screwed Molly's face in knots. "Nothin'. Just sat there on his horse staring. He finally gritted out, 'Don't start preaching at me,' and took off like a black streak, as if the Devil himself was chasing him."

Never had Chantel worked harder than that spring of 1883. She insisted on learning everything there was to know about ranching. The calves that had been dropped during the winter had to be branded. She hated the stink of burning hides but forced herself to watch as the Triangle C was applied with the red-hot branding iron. She could throw a saddle on Chinook and cinch it tightly, after remembering to shove her horse in the ribs so he wouldn't swell up on her and spill her out of a too-loosely girthed saddle. She could ride like an Indian and even shoot straight, although she never slipped the little gun in her blouse without distaste. Yet she was not coarsened by her new skills. The Montana sun tanned her, bringing wild roses into rounder cheeks caused by Molly's good food.

Memory of the ransom threat dimmed before the daily routine. She had no time to worry; there was too much to be done. Over Molly's and Santa Fe's protests, she refused to wait around for an escort to take her riding. "No one's going to bother me," she insisted. "The whole countryside knows our boys would take to their saddles if anything happened to me!"

Santa Fe scratched his head and reluctantly agreed. "That's for sure. But I still don't like it."

Chantel pulled his hat down over his eyes and laughed, continuing to ride when and where she chose.

Letters had come to the Triangle C. Mr. Barker wrote to say that Chantel's grandmother's legacy was still being debated. Chantel read more between the lines than in what he actually said. She had hesitated a long time, but she finally sent a brief Christmas greeting to Lydia and Anita, with no message for Arthur. It was just a simple statement that she was well and happy and hoped they were the same. There had been no response. The intervening months had softened Chantel toward her tormentors. She could only feel pity, especially for Anita. If only the girl had known a different way of life, perhaps things would have been other than they now were. Had Arthur and Anita married in the year since Chantel had been gone?

"I hope not," Chantel told Molly. "He can never make any woman happy." She'd told Molly the whole story in pieces and snatches over the winter.

"Too bad she can't meet a real man," Molly agreed slyly. "Like Brand or Duke."

Hot protest rose in Chantel, then she laughed at Molly's knowing look. "Yes, isn't it?" She couldn't help wondering how immaculate Anita would fare in the west, or how Brand and Duke would react to the blond beauty.

One late afternoon Rosy rode in with the mail from town. Chantel was delighted to discover a fat letter from her train friend, Serena Farley. Her eyes sparkled as she opened it and read the first paragraphs. "Molly, she wants me to go visit her."

"Are you going? If so, now's a good time. You've got me and Santa Fe hitched, and the boys are getting the cattle moved up to better grass. Canning and preserving won't start for awhile."

"I'd love to see her again." Wistfulness for the first friend she'd made in Montana Territory colored her face with longing. "I can take the train to Butte. She'll get there and meet me. She hopes I can stay at least a month."

"Makes sense, after a long trip like that." Molly's shrewd glance approved. "Why not go? Write back and tell her you're coming."

Chantel was still dubious. "You really think I should?"

"Seems to me it'd be a good thing. You've scarcely been off the spread since you came. In Missoula you can meet folks and have some fun."

"All right." Chantel wrote her letter and dispatched it with one of her hands. The next two weeks were spent repairing clothing and selecting what she'd need for her visit. She could barely control her excitement. The trip west had been marred by fear of what lay behind, but this trip promised nothing but pleasure.

What perverse imp prompted Chantel to caution Santa Fe and Molly not to mention her trip to Brand if he rode over she didn't even understand herself. Unless it was that he might think she was deserting now that the first flush of owning the Triangle C had subsided. Even so, whenever the drumming of horses' hooves sounded she changed color. She'd tried and tried to put him from her mind, to no avail. She had berated herself for foolishness, and it did no good. His image haunted her dreams, rode with her on the trails. It would be good to get away completely for a time and force herself to forget his attraction.

The visit did not solve her problem. Although she flew to Serena Farley like a homing bird and even enjoyed the creaking stagecoach ride to Missoula, part of her cried out for the Triangle C and all that had grown so dear. She missed the familiar, and at the end of two weeks apologized to Serena and sent a message that she was on her way home.

"I understand, child." The older woman's eyes were kind. "I'd like to hold you, but your heart's down there." With Serena's blessings, and under the watchful eye of the stage driver, Chantel endured the ride bodily, while her mind soared ahead. What was happening on her ranch? Had the rustlers Brand expected been at work? Dread shot through her. In vain she tried to reassure herself. She'd been gone only a short time. Surely nothing terrible had happened. Yet cold, unreasonable fear had taken possession of her. She was glad to climb down from the rocking coach at Butte and see everything was just as it had been when she left. Now just a train journey home!

"Miss Evans?" A cowboy with hat pulled low accosted her as she started toward the train depot. The genial stagecoach driver had delivered her practically there.

"Why, yes." She didn't recognize him.

"I'm sorry to say your foreman Santa Fe's been hurt. Would you come with me, please?"

A sickening rush of the same fear she'd known earlier threatened to overpower her. "What happened?" She peered more closely into his face. "And who are you?"

"I'm Slim Aiken. Santa Fe put me on

just after you went to visit."

He'd said they'd be needing extra help, Chantel remembered, even as she asked again, "But what happened to Santa Fe?"

Slim took her arm. "We have to hurry." He led her toward a team and buggy where the driver was impatiently flicking his reins. "A band of rustlers came down against some of the Triangle C hands. Must have thought they'd surprise us. Santa Fe let out a bellow and rode after them. The rest of us was trying to stop the stampede when the rustlers had fired shots in the air. We heard shots in the distance, and when Santa Fe didn't come back, we followed. He's shot up pretty bad."

Chantel couldn't grasp the full significance. "But why are you here? They knew I'd be coming in on the train."

"Molly reckoned it would be faster if I met you here." He hurried her into the buggy and sprang in after her. "Driver, make tracks!"

Something inside Chantel stirred — a faint flicker of suspicion. "Molly sent you?" Why hadn't she sent Brand or Duke, or even Rosy?

"Yes. Molly McLeod herself."

The warning twinge grew louder. "How long have you been on the Triangle C?"

She tried to see his eyes beneath his hat brim.

"Since the day after you left."

Then why had he called her Molly McLeod, instead of Molly Jones? The whole countryside knew her and Santa Fe had married. "Driver," she called sharply, "turn back. I prefer to go by train."

The smooth voice of the man beside her changed to roughness. "Sorry, Miss Evans, I was told what to do. You're coming with us."

The next moment a cloth was thrown over her head. A faintly sweetish odor assailed her nostrils. She tried to fight, to throw it off, but a strange lassitude paralyzed her muscles. Then all went black.

PART III

10

Brand Morgan dispiritedly turned Dark Star toward home. He was tired, tireder than he'd been in years. For five nights he'd lain in hiding, waiting for the band of rustlers who should have responded to reports he'd secretly circulated about the new herd on the Rocking M. Nothing had happened. Was there a traitor in his selected band of men? He mentally reviewed them — tanned, smooth, or grizzled faces, young and middle-aged — then shook his head. He'd stake his life on them.

But it wasn't the sleepless nights that haunted him. He'd ridden faster and harder before. It was beginning to show, too. His foreman, Carson, had complained, "What's eatin' on you, boss? You're touchier than a long-tailed coyote in a room full of rockin' chairs."

Carson wasn't noted for his perception. Brand's misery must be plainer than Eagle

Peak on a clear day, for Carson to see it.

Dark Star slowed her pace, but her rider never heeded. When had he started no longer caring what happened to the Rocking M he'd slaved and sweated for, jealously guarding against the elements and raiders? Or did he still care, but couldn't concentrate because of something looming larger than even the Montana thunderheads above the mountains?

"Might as well admit it, old girl," he absently stroked Dark Star, whose ears perked up. "Ever since the old man's granddaughter showed up, I've been off my feed and acting as if I'd eaten loco weed."

He laughed harshly, striking a discordant note in the early dawn air. How he'd fought it, cursing himself for a fool. He was no peach-fuzz kid to moon around over a girl; he was going on thirty-two.

"Probably just struck because I never had time for girls before," he soliloquized, his keen eyes watching the glow behind the butte that heralded the approach of day. "Been too busy getting established, Star." He barely heard Dark Star's gentle nicker. Even piling up everything he knew against her was useless. All his accusations, suspicions, and disgust had been swept away the reckless night months ago when he swept aside her defenses and kissed her. The touch of her soft lips against his own had done what he'd thought nothing could do: set a fire blazing in his heart that time and fighting couldn't put out. It was worse than a prairie fire, always racing ahead and breaking out where least expected. He'd made up his mind that women were more trouble than they were worth — then she came. Chantel. Her name sang in the night winds. She'd spoiled his enjoyment of even the Rocking M. Every deep pool of water or dark, forested glade echoed her eyes. The sheen of Dark Star's coat when brushed reminded Brand of Chantel's dark hair. The early June wild roses were but pale shadows of her glowing cheeks.

Was this what Charles Evans had meant when he'd said the first Chantel had given him everything a man could want? Brand remembered how he'd secretly scorned the old man, powerful in the knowledge that he himself had carved out all he wanted. What an arrogant fool, to tempt fate by declaring himself out of range of love. Now, in spite of his vow to tear this thing from his life, unwanted visions of her before the fire at the Rocking M, a curly-headed child in her lap, rose to remind him how empty his life had become. At times he hated her for ever coming. Better never to have known this feeling than to know and be forever barred from her love. And he was.

She was a Christian. Even if the barrier of east-west could be broken down — and according to Santa Fe that was just what Miss Boss was doing — there remained the invincible barrier of her beliefs.

"If You're really there, the way she believes," he flung to the heavens, "You're probably laughing Your head off. What could be a better punishment than having me building prairie dreams about her?"

There was no answer. He had expected none. A God who mocked him by letting him get in this mess wouldn't bother to answer.

"She'll probably turn Duke soft and marry him." Why not take comfort in that thought? It would serve Duke right, the way he'd thrown away their friendship.

The gate of the Rocking M showed ghostly in the first streaks of daylight before he straightened. He wearily led Dark Star through instead of jumping it, as they usually did. He was in no mood for anything but bed. Yet after rubbing down his faithful horse and climbing into bed, sleep didn't come. He tossed restlessly for an hour, then got up, washed, shaved, and dressed in clean clothes. By the time Ah Soong had ham, eggs, and biscuits ready, Brand had already been to the bunkhouse and given orders to his hands to keep their eyes and ears peeled.

"Got enough of that for one more?" Santa Fe licked his lips and grinned from the doorway.

"You bet." Brand waved him in. "Didn't hear you ride up."

"Must have something on your mind." Santa Fe shoved his sombrero back from his sandy hair, took the plate Ah Soong handed him, and lavishly loaded it. "That cooky of yours sure can cook." He hastily added, "Not like Molly, but good."

"Just what are you doing here this time of day?" Brand buttered a biscuit and cut through Santa Fe's rambling. "I've never known you to pay a social call when there's a brand-new day of work to be done." He surveyed Santa Fe with a steady gaze. "Nothing wrong at the Triangle C, is there?"

"I don't know."

"Don't know?" Brand glared at him. "If you don't know, who does? Or has the boss fired you?"

"Don't get riled. She ain't fired me. She ain't even there."

A trickle of foreboding washed down Brand's spine. His hands clenched on his knife and fork. "Where is she? Gone back to Boston?"

Santa Fe's face turned red. "Course not! Can't you get it through your thick head she's staying? She went to Missoula to visit a woman she met on the train when she first came out here."

Relief flowed through Brand. "Then what's all the shooting about?"

Sante Fe wiped his lips and put down his cup. Brand had never seen quite the look that came to his friend's face: indecision, worry, and something indefinable mingled.

"That's just it. Maybe there ain't no cause. But I can't help feeling something's wrong." His keen eyes flashed. "Molly says I'm borrowing trouble, but Molly don't know all I do." He took a dirty envelope from his pocket.

Santa Fe unfolded it, then said, "There was a letter to me in it. From Miss Chantel."

"So what? Isn't it natural she'd write? How long has she been gone? Why didn't I know about it? Why get het up over an envelope?"

Sante Fe held up a protesting hand against the barrage of questions. "First off, she had some queer notion about your not knowing. I feel I'm breaking a promise to tell you, even though it was Molly what said we'd keep still. Next, she's been gone almost a month, just like she said she'd be."

"I can't see anything suspicious about that. What did she say in the letter?"

"That's just it. There ain't no letter." Sante Fe tapped the torn envelope.

"You're not making sense!"

"I've sense enough to know it's funny that this empty envelope should be found wadded up under one of the bunks, instead of having been delivered to me right and proper."

"Whose bunk?"

"Drifter named Aiken. Rode in one evening a few weeks ago, saying he needed work. We're full-handed, so I told him sorry, we'd hired all the extra help we needed, but he was welcome to bed down overnight. He acted appreciative and rode out the next morning."

"When was the envelope found?" Tiny spurts of alarm twanged Brand's nerves.

"Yesterday. Molly stuck her head in the bunkhouse and couldn't stand the mess, so she up and tackled it. She had everything stacked up for burning, and when I packed it out for her, I saw my name."

The spurts settled into a steady throb. "What have you done about it?"

"Sent Rosy to Dillon to see what he could find out. Told him to meet me here as early as he could get back this morning."

"So we wait."

"Yeah." The keen eyes pierced Brand. "Thought you oughta know, you being so crazy about my boss and all."

Angry streaks of color shot into Brand's set face. "That's none of your business, Santa Fe. Get me?" His voice was deadly.

"Sure. Never did stick my nose in other folks' affairs. Just kept it out and let it grow." He patted his hawklike nose affectionately.

Brand couldn't help laughing in spite of his irritation. He must be wearing love like a pair of chaps for everyone to see. On the other hand, Santa Fe was so downright smug over marrying Molly he probably saw romance hanging on every sagebrush.

It was almost noon before Rosy rode in on an exhausted horse. "Water!" he gasped as he slid from the saddle. "Didn't stop to drink on the way." He gulped great dipperfuls before tersely saying, "Terrible trouble."

In the heartbeat while the boy caught his breath, Brand braced himself for what was to come.

"Rode in and saw the mail carrier. He remembered giving a letter from Miss Chantel to a rider who said he was heading our way — a slim, good-looking dark feller. It came just after our boys'd been in for the mail, and he figured he'd like it right away. Said if he'd known the stranger wasn't all right, he'd never have let him take it. But the rider said he knew Molly and Santa Fe and would be glad to fetch it. He'd even asked if there was any Rocking M or Circle Four Peaks or Triangle C mail."

"Aiken." Santa Fe confirmed sourly.

"That ain't all." Rosy produced another letter from inside his shirt pocket. "This came for Miss Chantel, and I took the liberty of opening it when I saw it was from Missoula."

"Read it," Santa Fe ordered.

"It's bad news," Rosy warned, then read:

Dear Chantel,

I plumb forgot to give you that recipe for hush puppies last week before you left, so here it is. Hope you can come again. Sorry you got homesick and went home early.

Affectionately yours,
Serena Farley

"Last week!" Santa Fe grabbed the note. "And look." He pointed to the smudged date. "This must have been at Dillon awhile." He drew out the torn envelope in Chantel's writing. "I bet this was to tell us she was coming ahead of time."

"Then she's been gone from Missoula for two weeks!" Rosy burst out.

"Did you learn anything else at Dillon?" Brand's face knotted.

"I asked the station agent how Miss Chantel looked, all decked out for her visit. He said she was 'purty as a pictoor,' standing there waiting to board the train for Butte." His eyes looked sick, and there was no suggestion of the color in his drawn cheeks that had earned him his nickname. "So she didn't get back as far as Dillon."

"I reckon we'll be riding then." Santa Fe swung his gun belt a bit higher on his lean hips.

"I'll go and take Rosy." Brand was rewarded by the gratitude in the boy's face. "It'd scare Molly to death if you up and took off."

"What're you aiming to do?" Santa Fe wanted to know.

Brand's eyes hardened. "Find her. We'll ride to Dillon, catch the train for Butte, wait and talk to the agent there, then the stage driver to Missoula. While we're gone, send out men and see if you can round up Aiken. If you find him, don't shoot him. We've got to know who put him up to collecting that letter, then riding out to Triangle C looking for a job, and maybe some information."

"They — whoever it is — won't hurt her, will they?" There was a sound suspiciously like a sob in Rosy's subdued voice.

"Why should they?" But the look Brand exchanged with Santa Fe belied his answer.

There was no more to be learned at Dillon than Rosy already knew. Brand and Rosy wasted no time there, boarding the train to Butte. Every clack of the wheels rang in Brand's heart like the sound of disaster.

Rosy took one look at the older man's face and subsided. Their trip was devoid of conversation, and Brand's active imagination played havoc. Why had she been waylaid? No ransom note had appeared. It would be better for Chantel if one had. Brand shuddered, remembering isolated incidents of abductions and the dulled eyes of one girl he'd seen who had been rescued. God forbid any such thing happened to Chantel! He wasn't even aware of the unusual wish. All he wanted was to find her. If money could do it, he would spare nothing.

They had a wait in Butte before locating the stage driver who'd been in charge of Chantel. When they did find him, there was little he could tell them. Yes, he'd driven when Miss Evans traveled from Missoula a couple of weeks before. Yes, he'd even taken her to the train depot. She was such a nice girl that he'd made sure she wouldn't be inconvenienced any. Yes, he'd seen someone come for her. Near as he could remember, it was a slim, good-looking cowboy. They'd climbed into a buggy hitched to the prettiest pair of matched bays he'd seen in a long time.

Matched bays. A light flickered deep in Brand's brain, then was immediately extinguished. Duke Price wouldn't dare abduct Chantel! There were more pairs of matched bays than his. Yet it was the only lead they had. The station agent at Butte was positive Chantel had not ridden his train to Dillon. The train crew was equally positive. They remembered her going to Butte, but she hadn't returned on *their* train.

How could a girl as noticeable as Chantel Evans simply vanish, and why?

Brand and Rosy left Butte and Dillon no nearer the answer than when they'd gone. Santa Fe had uncovered nothing about Aiken, either, and Molly was wild.

"If I get my hands on that skunk —" Her Irish eyes glowed with passion. "I'll —" a tear drowned the rest of her threat.

"It's been three weeks." Santa Fe's usually jovial face was glum. "And we're no better off than we were then!" He turned away, but not before Brand caught the working of his face. "On top of it, the boys reported someone drove off a hundred cattle from the west range last night. Couldn't track 'em. Can you beat it? A hundred cattle gone, and no sign!"

"There wouldn't be, if they were driven up Bannock Creek, then across that hardpan to the hills," Brand replied. "Get your boys out in the morning, Santa Fe, and head straight for Eagle's Peak." He paused. "I think I'll pay a little call on Duke Price."

"Good idea," Santa Fe approved. "What with the kind of men hanging around the saloon, he'd be likely to hear tales if anyone would." He shook his head. "He'd never stand for Miss Chantel being bothered, but I ain't so sure he wouldn't appropriate some cattle."

All the way to the Circle Four Peaks, Brand framed what he'd say to Duke. He could have saved the effort. His men reported that Duke hadn't been around for a couple of weeks.

Brand's elation was mingled with doubt. Coincidence? Mighty convenient. "How about my taking a look at his matched bays while I'm here? I've been wanting to trade off my team." He didn't miss the look two of the hard-faced men exchanged before one said in a bland voice, "Sorry, Mr. Morgan. We ain't got the authority to show the team."

Brand restrained an impulse to throttle the man and said indifferently, "I'll see Duke later."

"You do that," he was advised. There was nothing to do but mount Dark Star and ride away, but once he'd disappeared from sight over a low rise, he halted Star and hid her in a thicket of low-growing trees and brush. He wormed his way back, intending to see if the bays were stabled. Flat on his belly when he got to the barn, he inched forward and lay prone, hoping to overhear something.

Silence greeted him. Evidently the hands had gone on about their work. Checking to see that his gun was easy in his holster,

Brand crept through a dusty window into the big barn. At first he was disappointed. Dark shapes shinnied from the far corner. So the bays were there after all.

"Get that barn mucked out!" The gruff order froze Brand. He mustn't be discovered here! Escape the way he'd come in was impossible. A shadow loomed in the doorway, cutting off that exit.

There was only one choice. He took the crude steps to the hay loft three at a time and dove headfirst into the loft. Heart pounding, he listened, then dared peek down. The crippled cowboy who took care of the stables shuffled below. Brand's breath returned to normal, and he crept across the loft and stationed himself near the wide, glassless window where the heavy shutter was fastened back to let fresh air into the hay. He'd hide until the barn was empty, or if he had to, he'd swing down the rope under cover of darkness.

Twilight had never lingered longer. Brand impatiently waited for enough darkness to cover his movements. The ranch was quiet, the house apparently deserted. The man below finished his work and left. Brand could hear his dragging feet. Good! Now was the time. He'd decided to use the rope. He started to swing it back and was stopped by a faint cry on the night breeze.

What was that?

His eyes fastened to a tiny light in the upper-story window of the house. Strange, the sound seemed to come from there. Or had he imagined it? He wiped sweat from his face and pulled back the rope.

The sound came again, as if someone in that room were crying. And it sounded like a woman's cry.

Jaw set, he made his decision. It was unbelievable that the sound was being made by Chantel Evans, but he could not leave until he knew. Soundlessly he slipped down from the loft, eased across the open space to the house, and stopped to reconnoiter. A light had sprung on in the lower part of the house. The smell of frying meat smote him, reminding him he hadn't eaten since breakfast. He stole closer and applied his eye to a crack in the curtain. A grumpy-looking cook was lifting steaks from his griddle, reaching a hairy hand toward the Dutch oven to lift it from the fire. As Brand watched, the man deftly added steaming biscuits to the plates. A door behind him opened, and his female counterpart joined him. The cook pointed to one of the plates and jerked a finger upwards. The next moment the woman disappeared from Brand's line of vision.

Brand sagged against the yellow pine tree behind him. Someone was being kept upstairs and served meals there. Who else could it be, except Chantel? He pushed down the fierce rejoicing inside. He would need the coolest head he'd ever possessed to carry out what he knew he was going to do. Rapidly, he planned. He could get the drop on the cooks and force them to hand over their prisoner. He shook his head. Not so good. If it wasn't Chantel, he'd have a hard time explaining to Duke Price why he'd held up his ranch.

Suppose he slipped in the back way and found his way upstairs? If the door was locked, he'd have to break it in, and the noise would draw attention.

He rubbed one hand against the other, finding them sticky with pungent pine resin. The next instant he started to climb. The limbs were sturdy for a way. If only they would remain so! He reached the window he'd observed earlier. The limb beneath him swayed dangerously, and he leaped to the sill of the open window.

For a single instant he stared at the girl frozen who slowly turned toward him. She must not cry out! He could hear the steady drum of hooves of the men coming back to the house from their work.

With a mighty bound, he was behind her. An iron-muscled hand clapped over her mouth. He turned her toward him and breathed, "Thank God!"

Eyes wide with fear, but apparently un-harmed, Chantel Evans looked up at him with growing recognition, and something in her eyes made Brand's heart rise to his throat and lodge there.

11

He had come, as she had known he would. Chantel opened her lips to repeat his thanks to God but was silenced by his shake of the head and low, "Don't make a sound!"

Heavy footsteps across the porch floorboards reminded Chantel of their perilous position. She quickly pushed Brand to the far corner of the room, behind where the door would swing open. She could see the protest in his face, and her eyes flashed with warning.

She was none too soon. One set of footsteps trailed up the rude stairs, and a thunderous knock came at the door. "You all right in there?"

It was a voice Chantel knew and dreaded. "Yes."

"Speak up." The knob rattled. A key began to turn, grating hard in the lock.

"God, help me!" Her whisper mingled with a rush of strength. Brand must not be found here. Either Aiken would kill him or Brand would kill her captor. She could read that in the eyes that had turned to molten metal in the lamplight. As the key finished turning and the door creaked open, she hastily unbuttoned the top button of her disheveled traveling dress, jerked her braids free, and feverishly loosened them.

"Don't come in," she ordered as haughtily as she could over the racing of her heart. "Here's the tray."

There was an awkward pause. Chantel's eyes never left Aiken's face. Admiration warred with some remnants of chivalry as he stammered. "I didn't know you were gettin' ready for bed." He removed his hat, accepted the half-eaten dinner on its tray, and backed away.

Chantel controlled an impatient desire to have him leave and smiled. "Good night."

"Good night, Miss Evans." He closed and relocked the door. Chantel pressed her face against it, hearing his booted feet clattering downstairs.

She never knew whether Brand moved with his usual catlike grace or if she turned to him, but she was in his arms, hot tears wetting his face as well as her own. Then the lips that had once hurled accusations at her claimed her own. Joy filled her, obliterating every doubt, even erasing the chasm between them created by his lack of faith in God. The protection of his arms was so welcome after her long ordeal! When he released her, she swayed toward him. "I knew you'd come."

A beautiful glow spread across his face, as she had seen the Montana Territory sunrise creep over the land, but he merely said, "Come." He led the way to the open window.

Chantel mentally checked the strength of the branch and the distance she was going to have to leap. She couldn't do it.

"There's no other way." Brand must have seen her dismay.

A vision of Brand facing the men below with blazing gun did what no amount of drumming up courage could have done. Her lips were whiter than her face, but she nodded.

"I'll go first." He swung out the window, anchored himself close to the pitchy tree trunk, and held out his hand. *"Don't look down."*

Lifting the heavy skirt of her dress and stepping to the sill, Chantel could discern Brand only as a black mass against the tree trunk. "Blow out the lamp," he directed. She obeyed, then allowed her eyes a few minutes to adjust. When she reopened them, she was amazed to see there was enough light from the stars to see his hand reaching for her. His fingers settled over her hand and wrist like talons. He would never let her go. She measured the distance and trembled, knowing she must do it! Was it for this moment that all the weeks of riding and hardening she'd gone through had prepared her? She poised, then jumped into what looked like endless space. A limb cracked, she slipped, then those rescuing hands drew her so close to him that she could feel his heart beating. Her involuntary cry was muffled against his massive chest.

"What was that?" The outcry was followed by clinking spurs as a man stepped to the yard below.

"Aw, Aiken, you're always hearing things," someone drawled. "C'mon back in. Supper's getting cold."

"Thought I heard something in the trees out here." Chantel could see his dark figure move to the base of the tree as Brand flattened himself and pulled her closer.

"You're spooked," the same drawling

voice accused. "The girl said she was going to bed, didn't she? She sure ain't going to be crawling around in trees." His sally brought a wave of jeering laughter, and Aiken went back in. The slamming of the door cut off a curse in the middle.

"Now." With incredible gentleness, Brand helped her down the tree. "Wait here."

Chantel found the short wait worse than anything she'd endured. Crouched under the frail protection of a cluster of small alders, she lived through torture until Brand returned. His fingers on her wrist sent tingles of relief through her. Silently they crawled away, until the light from the ranch house no longer touched them.

"Can you ride in that dress?" Doubt colored Brand's question.

"I'll have to." Chantel repressed a nervous laugh and clumsily climbed onto the horse he led close. "Is it Dark Star?"

"Yes. The nag I borrowed won't be as fast. If we're chased, lean low and call in Star's ear. She'll outrun any rider in Montana Territory."

His voice sent chills through her. "And what will you be doing?"

"I'll stop anyone who tries to stop you."

"No!" Chantel's fear for him was greater

than for herself. She relied on the only thing she knew to prevent tragedy. "I don't know my way. You must stay with me." She could see his face gleaming in the starlight. "If I run Dark Star and she falls, I could be killed."

For a moment she thought he would resist, but then his quiet voice instructed, "Follow me."

Slowly at first, then at a faster pace once they were out of earshot, their night ride was strange. Chantel asked at one point, "Shall I tell you what happened?" but Brand shook his head. "Not now. There'll be time for that later." She could see in the starlight how the scar on his face stood out on his face. His chiseled features were cold and hard. It was difficult to believe that the radiance that had warmed them earlier had ever existed.

But Chantel had enough to do without taking time for reflection. Cumbered by her traveling dress, she longed for the freedom of her well-worn deerskin riding suit. When the sound of distant horses first reached them, she longed for her riding clothes even more. "Is it them?"

"I don't know." Brand reined in his mount and listened, then shook his head. "No. Wrong direction, but there's a bunch of riders coming hard. We'll get off the trail until we find out who they are. Stay on Star. We may have to ride in a hurry."

What new menace was this? Chantel wondered. Even the stamina she'd built up since coming west was starting to fail. The shock of her abduction, followed by restless nights and fear-filled days, had taken its toll. She was gradually numbing to where nothing mattered. She drooped in the saddle as Brand slid to the ground and held the horses' heads so they would not whinny.

The riders came nearer, a strangely silent bunch of men. Chantel counted twelve as they swept past and was startled when Brand cried out, "Santa Fe. Pull up!"

"That you, Brand?" Affection and relief mixed in the bellow. "Where you been?"

"I've got Chantel."

In spite of her weakness, she couldn't miss the reverence in Brand's voice.

"Good. We've got our rustler. Your old pard Duke."

Brand leaped into the trail and walked up to the riders. "Is that true?" His words lashed like a whip. "Where?"

Santa Fe's voice oozed satisfaction. "Just like you said. The Triangle C cattle had been driven up Bannock Creek, across the hardpan to Eagle Creek. Purtiest little setup a man could ask for — and Circle Four Peaks brands all over the place." Santa Fe hesitated. "Found Duke drinking coffee in a shack someone's thrown up there."

"So you are a rustler, as well as an abductor of an innocent girl."

"Hang him!" a voice called from the rear.

"Good idea," another chimed in.

Chantel fought her paralyzing fear. "No! You must not do this terrible thing!" She touched Dark Star lightly in the flanks and she sprang forward, scattering riders. "I don't know he was responsible for my being taken."

"Even when I found you captive on his ranch?"

She hated Brand's skeptical tone of voice. "Whatever he is, he deserves a fair trial." She appealed to Santa Fe, knowing that trying to change Brand's mind would be useless.

"You don't understand, Miss Chantel. In this country, cattle thieves deserve hanging. They're like wolves, sneaking in to raid and take food from honest men who've worked hard."

She stared at him in the dim light, unable to grasp how he could sit there so calmly. "You're a Christian and you can say that?" She could see his eyes turn away and pressed the point. "If he's proven guilty, the law will take care of him. You men must not have his blood on your hands!" A surge of power brought her erect in the saddle. "Santa Fe, for the first time, I'm overruling one of your orders. Take Duke to Dillon and see he's turned over to the sheriff."

Could that be relief in Santa Fe's face?

He replied, "You're the boss," and ordered, "Duke, if you try anything, we won't get to Dillon."

"Want some of us to go with you?" Rosy had ridden forward with the prisoner.

"Won't be necessary." Santa Fe prodded Duke's horse, and they disappeared into the darkness.

Duke hadn't said one word, Chantel realized. How peculiar! Brand must have thought so, too, for he said, "Something funny's going on," and stared after the departing men with narrowed eyes.

"Please, can we go home?" The inevitable letdown threatened to unseat Chantel.

Brand swung back to her. "Of course." His gruffness failed to hide his concern. "Can you make it?"

"Yes." Every ounce of willpower she possessed was used to show the men that she was not a weakling. She would make it, with the help of God.

She did. Although barely aware of reaching the Triangle C and being lifted from the saddle by Brand, triumph raised the heavy veil of weariness long enough for her to assure Molly she was all right and promise, "I'll tell you everything tomorrow." It was the last thing she knew until an eternity later, when she heard someone say, "Duke got away from me!" She roused. Santa Fe must have come back.

"Made it nearly to Dillon, and he was no trouble at all. Asked polite-like if he could stop for a drink at the stream. Climbed down and spread flat. I reached for my canteen, and he jumped me, took away my gun, and said, 'Sorry, Santa Fe. No jails for me.' Last I seen of him was his hat bobbing along the mesa from where he left me. Took me an hour to catch my horse. Duke'd let him go."

Gladness washed through Chantel. No matter how bad Duke was, he'd been good to her. Any western jury would be hard on a rustler. Maybe he'd go away and make a fresh start somewhere. She hoped so. But even her relief over his escape wasn't proof against her own exhaustion. She closed her eyes and slept again.

The second time she awoke, she was clearheaded and conscious of a gnawing feeling in the pit of her stomach. She lay still a few seconds, reveling in her own freedom and the sunshine making fantastic patterns on her walls. She wrinkled her brow, puzzled. Why was the sun coming in that window? What time was it, anyway?

The door quietly opened and Molly peered in. "Oh, you're awake. Good. The sheriff's here. And that ain't all." She handed Chantel a plate of toast and jam. "This will hold you until supper."

"Why so mysterious? I suppose the sheriff's here to see what happened to me." Chantel was already biting into the toast.

The cloud on Molly's face didn't lift. "Get dressed fast. Trouble always comes in threes."

Chantel was still too listless to care what new doom Molly was predicting. Probably more cattle were gone. At least she was safe. She reached for a simple summer cotton, pale yellow, to give a bit of brightness to her sagging spirits. After so many days in the traveling dress, it was good to be clad in a lighter gown.

They were all gathered in the big room waiting for her: Brand, Santa Fe, Molly, the sheriff, even Rosy.

"Now, Miss Evans, tell us exactly what happened, from the beginning." The persuasive voice relaxed Chantel.

"There isn't much to tell. I missed the Triangle C." Her eyes flew to Brand, who sat impassively watching her as if no tender moments had ever passed between them. Her face burned, and she forced herself to continue. "He — Aiken — told me Santa Fe had been hurt and Molly sent him for me. He had a buggy and a driver waiting. He said we had to hurry, and that Molly McLeod wanted me to go with him." She hated herself for stammering like a schoolgirl.

"The skunk!" Santa Fe interrupted. He settled back at a glance from the sheriff.

"I remembered he said he'd come to work at the Triangle C just after I left. I started getting suspicious. If he'd been here two weeks, he'd have known she was Molly Jones. I called to the driver to turn back. Aiken threw a cloth over my head. It smelled sickening, a little sweet." She clenched her hands, remembering with horror what came next.

"When I woke up, I was in an incredibly

212

dirty room. Yet the walls looked new. There was a pitcher of water, and I tried to bathe. Hours later Aiken came. He looked strange. His eyes glittered. He never touched me, but I was afraid. He told me I was his ace in the hole. I wouldn't be harmed unless a certain somebody refused to carry through. I didn't know what he meant. I asked where I was. He said in the back of the Chantel saloon." Her voice broke.

"I knew we shoulda burned that hellhole up!" Santa Fe burst in.

"How did you get to the Circle Four Peaks ranch?" the sheriff wanted to know. "And when?"

"Not for over a week. Then I heard some man tell Aiken it was too risky keeping me there. That night they tied and gagged me and put me in the same buggy that had been at Butte." Her eyes closed against the surge of agony that rushed back. "I prayed to die rather than be taken to some lonely shack! I asked God to send someone to help me."

"Did you ever see Duke Price?"

"No." She was positive about that. "He wasn't home."

"Reckon he wasn't," Santa Fe put in. "Too busy rustling cattle. He must of figured we'd be so worried over you being missing that we'd be careless about keeping an eye out for the stock."

"Anything else?" the sheriff persisted.

"No. Except once I got to the ranch, the cook and his wife let me walk outside during the day while the hands were working. I wasn't allowed near the barn, and if I got more than a few feet away from the ranch house, they made me come back."

"Who did you see besides those two?"

"Old Charley, the stable hand, and Aiken. He came every night to see how I was." Flaming color crept to her hairline. "He never was anything but courteous, in his rough way." She felt she had to explain. "I'd feared. . . ." She couldn't finish.

The sheriff lumbered to his feet. "I'll just mosey over there and see who's around." He eyed Chantel keenly, and she was impressed by the intelligence in his weathered face. "Firebrand's already told me how you escaped. Do you have anything to add?"

"Yes." They were all looking at her, waiting. "Mr. Morgan may not know or believe it, but he came because God sent him. I prayed for deliverance. I asked God to send a rescuer." Chantel saw a tiny pulse start beating in Brand's face, the only sign of emotion in his carefully masked countenance. It gave her the courage to speak for her Lord. "I claimed the promise as a child of God through Jesus Christ — and He answered."

With an inarticulate sound, Brand bounded from his chair and out the open door. Chantel could hear Santa Fe's hard breathing in the stillness of the room. Molly was frankly wiping her eyes. Rosy smiled at her, then looked down at his boot, which was scuffing the bearskin rug.

"Well." The sheriff broke the silence. "I know it wasn't easy for you to have to tell it all over again, Miss Evans, but we'll try and catch Aiken." He cleared his throat. "Also Duke."

"Remember, he wasn't around," Chantel pleaded. "There's something odd about Duke and the missing cattle. I can't figure it out, but I still don't believe he's crooked."

"I caught him myself," Santa Fe reminded grimly, with a furtive look at the sheriff, whose pupils had dwindled to pinpoints.

Chantel spread her hands helplessly. "I just can't believe we know everything there is to know. I don't even know why I was abducted or how long I'd have been held if Brand hadn't come!"

The sheriff played his trump card. "There's more to know than we've discovered, but I found out one thing. The man who calls himself Slim Aiken is wanted in Utah for large-scale rustling, and I wouldn't be surprised if he's the one who's been behind all the raids around these parts as well." A frown furrowed his face. "What I can't understand is why he was so free and easy with Duke Price's rig and team and ranch. Unless Price's the big boss behind him." His eyes returned to normal, and he smiled a crooked grin. "Thanks again, Miss Evans. The old man would be proud of you."

Chantel's heart warmed at his open approval. "Thanks, sheriff. That means a great deal to me." She sobered. "What's going to happen to Duke if he's caught?"

Surely the lightning glance in the big man's eyes couldn't be fear! Yet the sheriff refused to look at her as he said, "I'm more afraid of what'll happen to him if he isn't."

His meaning was clear, and Chantel backed away from him. "I've ordered my men not to kill him!" She pressed her hands to her face.

"You can't order the Rocking M hands."

As if sorry he'd brought it up, the sheriff mumbled, "Besides, I'll get him first," and backed out the door.

Chantel staggered and dropped back into a chair. "Oh, Molly, this is a terrible land! What am I going to do? Killing and trouble and injuries. Will I never be free of them?" She waved toward the open door that framed a portion of the sky. Great storm clouds were gathering, as they had done so many times before. "They're beautiful, and terrible. They have followed me across the country. Will I ever escape the tragedies of this life? Or will they always be there ready to attack, the same way Satan attacks on every hand?"

Molly only reached out a strong hand and let Chantel cling to it.

"I thought God was leading me here, yet all the things that have happened since —" her voice trailed off.

"Have you changed your mind about your heavenly Father's loving care, Chantel?" The intensity of the query shocked Chantel into temporary speechlessness. Molly pulled her from her chair and to the front door. "You'd better not. Just look out there!"

Chantel shut her eyes hard. It must be a mirage, result of the strain she'd been under. She opened her eyes. This was no mirage, no figment of her overtired imagination. The figures were real, picking their haughty way to the porch, ignoring the gaping hands gathered for supper but entranced by the tableau.

"I told you trouble came in threes," Molly hissed. "You're going to need all the trust you've got."

Chantel didn't answer. She was too stunned by the group coming nearer.

Lydia, hair coiffed in spite of her surroundings, holding her stylish skirts high, crying, "Surprise, Chantel. Your family and fiancé have come to visit!"

Anita, gowned in what must be the latest Boston mode, raised appealing blue eyes and smiled into Brand Morgan's startled face.

Arthur Masters, resplendent in an easterner's conception of what cowboys wore, was totally unaware of what a ridiculous figure he presented next to the real cowboys now howling on the bunkhouse steps at his expense — and at the two guns worn low on his hips, tied down in imitation of notorious gunfighters.

12

For one rebellious moment, Chantel wondered if she should order them off the Triangle C or burst into hysterical laughter. She did neither. She simply opened the door wider and said, "I believe supper is almost ready. Won't you come in?" She smiled into Brand Morgan's face. "You too, Mr. Morgan."

Lydia's gasp was lost in Molly's approving whisper. "Good for you! Don't forget, you're mistress here," she said before she headed toward the kitchen.

Chantel's greeting set the tone for the endless days that followed. Her self-invited guests showed no disposition to leave, although Lydia disparaged everything about the ranch. "I can't see why your grandfather didn't modernize, with all the money he had."

"He liked it this way. So do I."

"And that impossible Mrs. Jones! You'd

better teach her that servants have their places. I asked her to bring my breakfast on a tray, and she told me either to eat with the rest or go without!" Lydia's blue eyes shone like hard sapphires, and she completely ignored the fact Molly was standing only a few feet away.

Chantel smiled at the remark and said, "Molly does know her place and fills it very well. She's my friend, not a servant." Lydia was effectively silenced.

Anita was in her element. The admiration of the cowboys had done much to turn her head. Once she told Chantel, "Arthur doesn't seem so big and important out here, next to some of your cowboys, does he?" Her eyes held the same look as her mother's. "Take Mr. Morgan, for example. If he could be tamed and taken east, he'd be a sensation. I might do just that!" She whirled away with an amazing flounce of skirts and a mocking laugh.

Chantel stared after her stepsister. There was no way she could have found out how Chantel felt about Brand.

Arthur Masters was profiting by his stay — literally. The first inkling Chantel had of trouble was Santa Fe's complaint. "There's going to be a fight, Boss. That whippersnapper comes sashaying into the bunkhouse, introduces some new card games only he understands, and fleeces the boys. They don't mind losing fair and square, but they won't stand for double-dealing, and even though he's a slick one, he's going to get caught."

"Oh, dear!" Chantel turned a miserable face toward Santa Fe. "What can I do?"

"Tie a tin can to them and ship 'em back east, before they ruin the outfit," was his terse advice.

Molly seconded him. "You're going to have to ask them to leave sooner or later, Chantel. They've settled in like buzzards over a dead carcass, and being polite ain't the answer."

Chantel sighed. She'd tried to be Christian about the whole thing, but it was getting out of hand. Why had they come, anyway? Her answer arrived in a fat packet of documents from Mr. Barker of Boston. He wrote that he now understood the whole situation. He wished she'd discussed it all with him, but he could see why she wished to keep private certain transactions of Mrs. Evans. The inheritance had been declared totally Chantel's. The house was hers, as well. If she could sign the papers in front of witnesses and return them, he would see that everything was taken care of.

So they had fled to Montana Territory for refuge because their claim against her inheritance was disallowed! Chantel was more amused than upset. But that didn't solve her problem. Santa Fe was right: Their presence was disturbing the work of the men. She must rectify it.

Days later she approached her guests, who were lolling in the shade of the tall, swaying cottonwoods to avoid the hot sun. "I don't mean to sound inhospitable, but what are your plans?"

"Well!" Lydia's mottled face warned of an impending storm. "A fine thing to ask!"

Chantel refused to be baited. "To be frank, your continued stay is creating problems here. My hands are not used to —" her eyes rested on the overdressed Arthur, "— to easterners. It's not long until we'll begin fall roundup."

"I've always wanted to see a roundup," Anita said eagerly.

"You'd hate it." Chantel smiled at the thought of exquisite Anita on a roundup. "Dust and sweat and burning hair."

"Don't be crude!" Lydia ordered with her old haughtiness.

"That's the way it is out here," Chantel confirmed, letting her gaze sweep the mountains in the distance.

"I've no intention of leaving." Arthur's lazy drawl, which had replaced his Boston accent, rang in Chantel's ears. "These clods are ripe for picking." He laughed contemptuously and twirled a gun. "I'm tucking away quite a chunk for after we're married, Chantel."

It was the first time he'd referred to the broken engagement, and Chantel turned scarlet with anger. "Sorry, Arthur." She stood. "I will never marry you." She caught a fleeting look of misery on Anita's face and throbbed with pity. Despite Anita's fancies toward cowboys, evidently she still loved Arthur.

Chantel took a long, deep breath. "Lydia, I am deeding the house in Boston to you. I'll never go back. It's to be given to Anita when you're finished with it. I'm fixing it so it cannot be sold, but will in turn go to her children, and theirs. I'm also requesting that you plan to leave here by the end of the month, two weeks from now." She ignored Anita's protest, Arthur's sullen twisting of his mustache, and Lydia's, "Well!" and continued. "I am planning a barbecue and exhibition of horsemanship as a farewell. It will be the night before you go." She turned and entered the house, followed by icy silence, then a muttered, "That seems to be that!" from Arthur.

Light running steps chased her down the hall, and she turned. Anita stopped before her, face flushed. "Chantel, thank you." Her husky whisper echoed in the hall.

Chantel caught the delicate hands, white even after Anita's riding. "Don't marry Arthur. He can never make you happy."

Anita's young, beautiful face sagged until she was suddenly old. "I will go through hell to have him."

"That's exactly where he will lead you." Filled with foreknowledge of what life with Arthur would be, Chantel shook the other girl lightly.

"It doesn't matter. At least I'll be with him," Anita sobbed. "You don't know what it's like to love someone so much you'd do anything to get him, even when you know what he's really like."

"Anita, that isn't love! God created love as something beautiful between man and woman, not an ugly, craving passion!"

"Don't preach to me, Chantel. I can't stand it. Do you think I like feeling this way, knowing if Arthur could get you and your inheritance, he'd never let up until he did?" Her face blazed. "Sometimes I hate him for what he is. Then he takes me in his arms and I know I'd do anything to keep him."

Revulsion swept over Chantel at the naked desire in the pale face before her. "Break free while you can. If you'll only ask God for help —"

"If there really is a God who cares the way you say, He'll make Arthur want me." Anita jerked free and ran down the hall into her own room, leaving Chantel shaken and nauseated by the scene.

It rose to haunt her over and over as Arthur made a last desperate bid for her attention and inheritance. He seized every opportunity to remind her of his devotion, openly bragging to the ranch hands how he'd change things when he was boss of the Triangle C, until Santa Fe reported, "That dude's going to get his head punched if he don't stop running off at the mouth."

Chantel patted his arm. "Just a few days and he'll be gone." She tried to divert his attention. "Anyway, the barbecue will be fun."

It started out that way. All afternoon, buckboards and spring wagons and buggies arrived. The neatly dressed women in calico and gingham dresses brought cakes and pies and pickles and vegetables, until the long board tables the hands had set up groaned under the weight of the offerings. Santa Fe presided over the whole cow that had been cooking slowly for hours, basting with a peppery sauce he said he'd learned to make when he worked a spell in Mexico. Laughter and tantalizing odors wafted across the ranch, enticing and proclaiming the day a holiday for as many hands as could be spared.

Chantel was everywhere, overseeing, lending a hand. Never had she been prouder than when her boys had practically swept the field of glory in the calf-roping, bulldogging, and various races. Only in the final horse race had they been outdone. Brand Morgan and Dark Star swept across the finish line a hundred yards ahead of the others, and Star didn't even act winded!

Chantel had handed Brand the twenty-dollar prize, saying, "She is the most beautiful horse I've ever seen!" Her sparkling eyes rested on the faithful black mare.

"She's yours."

Chantel turned back to him, wondering if she'd heard him right. "Mine?"

"Yes." A smile lurked in the golden eyes, setting her heart afire. "Of course, there's a condition. I go with her." He didn't wait for the reply she couldn't have made anyway, but led Dark Star away past the cheering crowd, leaving Chantel torn with love and the realization of how far apart they still were. But there was no time for introspection now. Santa Fe was bellowing, "Come and get it!" and the excited crowd pushed to the food tables and barbecue site.

"Chantel, may I speak to you a moment?" Lydia's eyes glittered strangely, as if she were distraught.

"Certainly." Chantel rose from her place on the blanket.

"Not here." Lydia looked nervously around. "Let's go out where your grandfather's buried."

Chantel was astonished but trailed Lydia, who kept looking back. "What is it?" she asked as Lydia stopped short.

"I've left my shawl, and it's chilly out here." Lydia shivered. "You were right about my wearing a low gown, but I did want to impress your friends." She broke off. "Go ahead. I'll just run back and be with you in a minute." Her bare neck and arms gleamed in the moonlight as she hurried to the ranch house.

Chantel couldn't stop a smile. Lydia would never know just how much of an impression she'd made with her unsuitable costume! Even Anita had been wise enough to stick with a simple, but well-cut dress.

Chantel lifted her own filmy skirts. Strange what a nuisance they were after wearing ranch clothing. She drifted on toward the cottonwood that sheltered the graves, wondering what Lydia wanted. Would she plead to stay? She had appeared resigned to leave, and their trunks were already packed. Chantel fervently hoped there would not be another scene.

A rustle in the leaves stopped Chantel. There was no wind. What was behind the tree? Unreasoning fear jolted her, and she forced herself to stand still. "Who's there?"

A gaudy figure, complete with satin shirt shining in the light and pearl-handled revolvers, stepped forward.

"Arthur!" Fear gave way to disgust. "What are you doing here?"

"Waiting for you." He came closer. "Lydia said she'd send you."

"So that's why she —" Chantel clamped her teeth in her lower lip. Arthur strode nearer. "She knew I needed to get you alone."

Chantel caught a whiff of his breath and turned her head in disgust. "You're drunk! I don't allow liquor on the Triangle C.

Where'd you get that?" She pointed to the bottle he held in one hand.

"Since you so admire western customs and all that, I thought I'd oblige." His words were a little slurred, and his burning eyes never left her face. "The Chantel saloon's not that far." His hands shot out. The bottle dropped, and his fingers dug into her arms through the frail protection of her thin sleeves.

"Take your hands off me!" Her dislike of the man reached feverish heights, but the fingers dug deeper.

"Why? I heard about your so-called abduction. So that's what they call it out here." He thrust his face closer to hers, and she shrank from the evil in his eyes and his whiskey-laden breath. "I also heard your captor was a pretty handsome guy. Don't tell me he didn't do a lot more than touch you, all that time you were gone!"

"*Let her go.*" The glacierlike cold voice came from behind her.

Chantel gave a cry of relief. Arthur swore and released her, venting his spleen on the intruder. "Who're you, to interfere with my fianceé and me?"

"That isn't true," Chantel whispered.

Enraged, Arthur swung back, reaching

for his gun. "I'll teach you!" He jerked the gun from the holster.

Chantel was swept aside as a pantherlike body hurled itself at Arthur. Before he could fire, the gun spun through space as Brand Morgan knocked it from his attacker's hand. The great Arthur Masters was pinned flat on his back, with a tawny body astride his midriff.

"Go back to your guests, Miss Evans." Brand's calm voice ordered.

"You won't —"

"I wouldn't waste a bullet on him. Now go."

Chantel fled, pressing her hands over her ears to shut out Arthur's craven, "Chantel, save me!" He had offered her the worst possible insult to womanhood. All her pleadings for him to be spared a licking would be useless, and she could no more stop the unleashed fury of Brand Morgan than she could stop an avalanche.

Somehow she managed to get to the house, bathe her face in cool water, and rejoin her guests. Brand was already there, mingling and smiling. She marveled at the changeability of him: One moment he was the defender, the next, the perfect guest. The only trace of the scuffle, if there had been any resistance on Arthur's part, which she doubted, was a slightly skinned knuckle.

Arthur didn't appear until the last guest had gone. He had evidently made what repairs he could, but one eye was swelled shut, and his face was scratched and bruised. His immaculate outfit had been discarded for a dark shirt and pants.

"Why, Arthur!" Anita flew to him in horror. "Whatever has happened to you?"

"Fell over some boards those idiot hands left piled up." He shot a baleful look at Chantel, who was staring at him. "I can hardly wait to leave this rotten country and get where people are civilized." He marched out.

A little later Anita said, "Arthur must have gone riding." Her face was wistful. "I saw him leading out a horse. I wish he'd asked me along." She sighed. "It's such a pretty night, so bright and all." Unshed tears misted her eyes. "I'm going to miss this." She straightened. "At least Arthur's gotten being a cowboy out of his system." A little smile crossed her lips. "Once I get him back to Boston, he's bound to settle down."

Chantel opened her lips, then closed them again. Anita had chosen; there was no use saying any more. "It's late, and we'd better get to bed." The evening had

drained her. "You have an early start tomorrow." She gave Anita a light hug and
was surprised at the girl's strong response.

"If it weren't for Arthur, I'd try and be
just like you," Anita whispered. Long after
Chantel retired for the night, she remembered the tribute. Perhaps she had at least
dropped a seed in Anita's life. God grant it
could sprout and grow, even in the rocky
path her stepsister was deliberately choosing. With a prayer on her lips, the tired
owner of the Triangle C dropped into an
uneasy sleep.

Her dreams were troubled. Anita called
for her, reaching out from some unknown
perilous place. Chantel's feet were lead.
She could not move. The dream changed.
Whispers in the hall were followed by
creaking leather and the sound of horses.

Chantel struggled free from the sheet
and sat up. Everything was still. Dawn was
cracking the sky into flaming segments.
Had it been a dream, or real? She snuggled
back under the covers, noticing how
summer seemed to have fled. Crisp early
fall air filled her room. She could still sleep
before it was time to be up and send off
the parting guests.

"Chantel!" Lydia's shriek echoed
through the ranch house. Roused from the

only deep sleep she'd had, Chantel leaped from bed and snatched a dressing gown. Barefooted, she ran down the hall to Anita's room, to find Lydia rocking back and forth on the bed, tears streaming down her face. "My baby, my baby!"

"Lydia, what's the matter?" Chantel demanded. The woman's tumbled hair and dull eyes predicted the worst.

"My baby, she's —" Lydia burst into wild sobbing. "It's all your fault!" She pointed an accusing finger at Chantel. "If you'd only married Arthur, this wouldn't have happened!"

"But what *has* happened?"

Lydia waved a piece of paper. "Anita's run off with Arthur, after all my planning." Anger was beginning to replace hysteria. "I've done it all for her, and she treats me like this!"

"Is that all?" Chantel was honestly shocked but relieved to discover things were no worse. She scanned the room and discovered a second folded piece of paper, addressed to herself. Some instinct cautioned her to read it before calling attention to her find. "Get dressed, Lydia. You still have a train to catch." She didn't heed Lydia's sputtering but ran lightly to her own room and opened the note.

Dear Chantel,

I'm marrying Arthur as soon as we can get to Dillon. It's the only way. Otherwise, Mother will never rest until she gets him married to you.

Arthur tapped at my door a few minutes ago. I've never seen him like this. He was absolutely wild, and demanded I elope with him. It must mean he loves me. He seemed absolutely terrified that we couldn't get away without being seen.

We'll meet Mother at the train station. Please, Chantel, pray for me. I'm almost scared of Arthur, even though he's all I've ever wanted. I haven't forgotten what you said and how I told you if there was a God, He could prove it by giving me Arthur. Well, He has. Sometime, after I'm old, I'll not care about parties and dances and fun, then I'll remember what. . . .

Anita

So the whisperings and sounds of horses had been real. Chantel was conscious of a great regret as she tucked the note into her bureau and hastily dressed. Anita had been near, but so far, from the Lord who loved her. Giving a few twists to her hair, she prepared for her final dealings with Lydia by dropping to her knees in prayer.

"It will be a tragedy only if you make it so," she told Lydia as Rosy helped the swollen-faced woman into the light carriage that would be most comfortable for the long ride.

"Won't you come with me?" Lydia in a pleading role was new to Chantel, but she shook her head. "It's better if I'm not there. You are the ones who will be living together, Lydia. If you don't make peace when you first are together, life will be unbearable."

"Thank you for the house."

It was the first acknowledgment of gratitude Lydia had ever shown, and Chantel responded graciously. "I believe it is what Father would have wanted."

A spasm of shame filled the reddened eyes. "He was good to me."

"He loved you, Lydia. He really did." Out of her suffering, Chantel had gained insight. "Even though he couldn't always express it freely, he cared."

"Good-bye, Chantel. You'll write, keep in touch?"

"Yes. God bless you, Lydia, and may you find happiness." Chantel watched the carriage out of sight, feeling as if a door had closed and locked on one part of her life. She had told them the truth the day she said she'd never go back. Montana Territory and the Triangle C had become home. On this cloudless morning it seemed that every trial was behind her.

She grimaced. Now only minor items such as rustlers, Slim Aiken, what would happen to Duke if he was caught, and her growing love for a man she daily prayed would come to honor her Lord were left to keep her from peace and contentment in her adopted land.

Yet, standing in the morning sunlight, hearing the cottonwoods whispering, and smelling the sagebrush, nothing seemed impossible. The inverted blue bowl of sky where an eagle soared and the far-off peaks lightly dusted with snow announced the coming of autumn and dying of the year, but the hope in Chantel's breast was for rebirth and life.

13

Firebrand Morgan headed Dark Star home, rubbing his skinned knuckle and grinning. He had been glad to leave the well-marked paths and homeward-bound conveyances. Dark Star was enough company for any man, especially when a never-ending round of scenes flickered in his mind. How beautiful Chantel had been in her thin gown, cheeks scarlet, dark hair done in a wonderful mass of curls on top of her head! His remark about his going with the gift of Star had struck home; he'd seen that in her pure face.

His face darkened and he gritted his teeth, remembering Arthur Masters taunting Chantel with vile, unspeakable things. He had wanted to kill him the way he'd killed a rattlesnake in the rocks a few days before. Even Masters's eyes reminded him of the snake, and the venom in his accusations was deadlier than the snake's. At least he'd stopped the sneering mouth. A few well-placed blows and the great eastern dude had sniveled and cried for mercy. Brand rubbed his hand again. It would be interesting to know how he'd explained his appearance, Brand thought, and smiled to himself.

When he reached the Chantel saloon, his smile faded. Even though dark and closed at this hour, it lay sinister and sleeping, like an evil beast that could spring alive and devour. Brand hated liquor. He'd seen enough of what it could do to men to stay clear. "One of these days I'm going to break loose and burn the place down," he promised. "Or make Duke do it." He rode on, face grim.

He felt it before he heard it — a scaring pain in his back, then the sound of a gunshot. He clung to Star's bridle in spite of the blackness that dropped over him, the sound of a second shot resounding in his ears. "Run, Star." He reeled in the saddle. Star lowered her head, flattened her ears, and ran. Behind him he heard a voice call, "Brand!"

Oh, God! So it was Duke. The tiny feelers of reaching toward God that had crept out before he found Chantel, and had been growing stronger since she told them he'd been sent to rescue her, died. To be killed at the hand of one he'd trusted and secretly hoped was innocent in the face of absolute proof of guilt was agony. No God would let such a thing happen, if He loved or cared about people, as Chantel believed. They were wrong, all of them: Chantel, Molly, Santa Fe, his own mother. He was right. There was no God, and never had been.

Through his pain, he clung to a single thought: He must remain conscious! Yet the time came when he could no longer hang on. Dark Star seemed to sense it and slowed, then stopped. Brand slid from the saddle, fighting nausea and waves of blackness. "Home, Star!" He slapped the mare on her rump. If Duke was trailing them, he'd follow Star. The horse snorted in surprise and hightailed it across the valley. Brand dragged himself off the trail and under a stand of alders. He could feel slippery blood when he reached over his left shoulder. Awkwardly, he ripped the bandanna from his neck and wadded it over the burning flesh on his back. The bullet must have lodged. Exploring fingers found no sign of a wound in his chest. Duke must have been a long way from him when he shot.

Duke! A fresh flood of misery swelled

through him. He closed his eyes and stretched flat so the bandanna would be pressed into the wound and stop the bleeding. Either he'd lay there and die with a bullet in his back or Duke would find him and finish him off! Either way, he'd hit the end of the trail.

He knew when he began to lose consciousness. Flashes from his past shimmered in front of his closed eyes: Charles Evans telling him he'd asked Jesus to be his pard. Chantel's unshakable belief that Brand had been sent as an answer to prayer. Molly's accrediting Charles's recovery to God's intervention.

"If only Duke hadn't . . ." he groaned. A half-forgotten memory from childhood swam before him. He stood at his father's knee, confessing some childish prank. He could even hear his treble voice excusing himself. "It was Abner who said we should do it." His father's exclamation cut through the explanation. "Son, what others do doesn't excuse you! Never let yourself think that someone else's sins justify your own wrongdoing."

He forced his eyes open, seeing the western stars glow above him. Was that what he'd been guilty of — blaming God because life had been hard? Was he deliberately refusing to have anything to do with a Creator who let people die, whether in war or from natural causes? What had Duke's shortcomings to do with his own responsibility? There under the alders, Brandon Morgan was forced to review everything he'd ever done. It wasn't pretty. Although he'd never consented to hanging or shooting anyone, hadn't he been guilty of setting himself up as ruler of his own creation?

The bullet wound had settled into a dull ache, but the pain in his heart rose to unbearable heights. Lately he'd wondered if God would forgive a rough rancher, even if he did repent. Now the cool night air painted pictures he'd sworn to bury forever, filling the injured man with remorse. An image of the curly headed child he'd been, kneeling at his bedside beneath a picture of Jesus, rushed out, no longer to be denied.

"Do you accept Jesus as your Savior, and promise to love and serve Him?" His mother's voice had been low. At the nod of his curly head, his mother had said, "Then tell Him about it."

"Jesus, I'm sorry for my sins. Forgive me and live in my heart."

A terrible groan sprang from the lips of

the suffering man. God! To have left that boy so far behind he didn't exist anymore. How could he have done it? Wait! Hadn't his mother said that once he confessed his sins, he belonged to Jesus? In spite of the way he'd marched away from that confession, had he broken the relationship? *Could* he declare he was no longer a child of God and make it stick, any more than Charles Evans, Jr., could when he cut loose? Charles had still been the old man's son, no matter where he went. Brand had left God and His Son; they hadn't left him.

"I'm sorry, God." The deep cry from his soul dwindled to a whisper. "It isn't because of Chantel. It isn't even because I'm probably going to cash in. Maybe You had to bring me down flat so I could see things straight. Forget all the things I said against You and remember I was smarter when I was a kid than I've been since." Poignant regret filled him, and a spasmodic twitch set the wound on fire again. "I just wish we'd had time to ride this beautiful land together, instead of me going it alone after Duke left." Something of the old resentment flared, and Brand added quietly, "It's none of my business about Duke. If You can forgive me, You could him, too." He desperately groped for shreds of awareness.

"Somehow, if Chantel could know. . . ." He jerked. The effort was too great. The stars were falling on him now. He closed his eyes and was still.

What was Santa Fe doing here? "Did he get you, too?" Brand muttered.

"Steady. Hold him still."

His back was on fire. How had he gotten turned over? There was something soft beneath his head. Funny, it wasn't crumbly like the aspen leaves. He was too tired to care. His throat was full of cotton. Had he gone back to Virginia? It was so hot! He thrashed about, panting. If only someone would give him water. A dark form loomed over him. "Drink this, Firebrand."

Duke! He convulsively grabbed the cup of water. "Shoot me, then bring me water." He laughed wildly. "You're a queer galoot, Duke."

A hard hand closed over his wrist. "Get this, Firebrand: *I didn't shoot you.*" Even through the red haze of fever burning him, Brand caught the sincerity. He made a feeble attempt to squeeze Duke's hand. They were pards now, riding and fighting together, building the Rocking M. But he had something to tell Duke. "We've got us another pard. Jesus. He'll be with us." He heard a gasp and relaxed, sinking into oblivion.

Darkness and heat. Were they waiting for the rustlers? "Don't hang him, take him to Dillon." Cold water being poured down him and over his face. More darkness, but he could see the outline of low hills to the east and streaks. The sun was coming up. Time to get started. Roundup was sunup to sundown. He struggled mightily and opened his eyes. Where was he? This wasn't his room.

"Welcome back, Brand." Duke? Where in thunder were they, anyway? He opened his mouth to ask, but no sound came.

"Don't try to talk. You were shot. I fished you out from under the alders and brought you to the Triangle C. Doc dug a bullet out of your back, but you've been out of your head with fever. We'll talk more when you're better." Duke handed him a cup of water. Brand drained it and closed his eyes again. This time there was no heat, just sweet sleep.

For three days Brand obeyed Duke's orders not to talk, but when he woke earlier than usual one day with a clear head and belly so empty he felt like a steer had caved him in, he couldn't stand it any longer. Duke appeared, smiling, tan and healthy, and Brand growled, "Enough coddling. I'm getting up."

"Fine. Doc said you'd be ornerier than a mother bear with cubs about the fourth day after you woke up."

"How long's it been?"

"Ten days since the barbecue." Duke grinned at the expression on Brand's face. "Let me whistle up breakfast."

"No more mush. I want a steak and biscuits!"

"You're better," Duke announced coolly, disappearing through the door and returning with Molly. "Says he wants a steak."

"Good." She grinned her Irish grin. "Sure, and it'll be cooked by the time you're ready for it."

"Can't see why a little old bullet should knock a man out so bad." Great beads of perspiration hung on Brand's face by the time Duke had helped him into clothes and a big chair by the window.

"That's what the trouble was — a little bullet that lodged, instead of going clean through you." Duke's lips were tight, his eyes slitted.

"Who shot me?" Their gazes locked.

"Arthur Masters."

"Masters! That eastern dude?" Brand ran one hand over his face, as if to clear the film from his eyes. "*He* knocked me out like this?"

"Near as we can figure. Remember those fancy revolvers he carried, kind of dainty-like? They'd be just about the right caliber. Besides, I saw him sneaking away from the Chantel saloon area just after the shooting." Duke's face was grim as he added, "I had to choose whether to go for him or follow you. I knew you were hit badly. By the time I found you and got you packed back here, Masters was long gone back east on the train. I figured I'd wait and see what you wanted to do about him."

"Let him go. I licked him for talking too free." A flash of understanding passed between them. "What I want to know is, where do you come into all this?"

Duke was saved by Molly and breakfast. Brand's mouth watered at the inch-thick beefsteak oozing juice onto the baked potato. "What? No biscuits?" He grinned at Molly.

"Chantel'll make some for supper." She flipped her white apron at him and taunted, "If she can stand looking at that grizzled face of yours." A laugh floated back from the hall as Molly left.

Brand ruefully rubbed one hand over his hairy face. "She hasn't been in here, has she, and seen me like this?"

"Molly?" Duke's eyes danced. "Sure,

and she's been my right hand." He caught Molly's inflection perfectly.

"You know who I mean." Brand looked daggers at Duke.

The mirth died from Duke's eyes. "She was here every minute when none of us thought you'd pull through. Molly finally sent her to bed after Doc said you were too tough to die. She's an angel if there ever was one here on earth." Duke's voice was husky.

"You're in love with her." Brand felt as if he'd been shot again. "And you must be straight, or you wouldn't be here." He took a deep breath. "Mighty nice of her to care what happened to me."

"She never quit believing you would live. When you hollered out that we'd got another pard, she looked like someone had handed her a little chunk of heaven." His dark eyes glowed like coals. "Any man who didn't love her would be loco, but it isn't me she cares for." He cleared his throat and brought a pan of water across the room. "Now let's get you looking human, instead of like some grizzly bear. The sheriff's coming this afternoon, and we'll wind up a few things."

Chantel nervously pleated the skirt of

her blue cotton dress as shuffling footsteps sounded in the hall. She hadn't seen Brand since he regained consciousness. Molly had advised her to let him take his time getting used to the idea of her having cared for him before meeting him face-to-face. Caring for a delirious man was one thing; going in after he was awake was another.

He was in the doorway now, leaning on Duke but searching for her. Color fluttered in her cheeks at his intent gaze, and she looked away, around the room she'd learned to love. The windows were open to let in the autumn air and sway the curtains. Sunshine mingled with the crisp air.

In some respects it was much as it had been the day after she was returned from the Circle Four Peaks ranch. Molly, Santa Fe, Rosy, Brand, and the sheriff were there. Only now Duke Price was present, guiding Brand to a chair. A moment of dread hovered, and Chantel sighed. What would the conversation disclose?

"Might as well get this meeting underway," the sheriff said. "Good to see you here, Brand." An affectionate look beamed from the sheriff's steely eyes.

"Good to be here."

His rich voice set Chantel's heart bounding. If Duke had been right and somehow that awful night of the shooting had brought Brand to the Master, as she'd prayed would happen, nothing stood between them and happiness. She put aside her dreams and listened. This was no time for building cloud castles.

"I suppose it all started about three years ago," the sheriff was saying. "Duke came to me, worried over the rustling that was going on. Seems he'd been approached by a certain Utah rustler anxious to get established in these parts."

"Aiken!" Brand spit out, his face darkening.

"Right. We agreed the best way to get the bunch of them was for Duke to play along. He didn't want to do it, first off." The sheriff glanced at him. "He hated the idea of appearing to double-cross Brand, and that's what he'd have to do. Finally I convinced him to talk it over with the old man and Santa Fe."

"Grandfather?" It was Chantel's turn to stare, red spots rising in her face. "He knew? Then that's why he apologized in the will." She caught her breath.

"Why wasn't I told?" Brand thundered, hands clenching. His golden eyes shimmered with anger. "All this time —" he choked.

"You're too hotheaded, pard." Duke's accusation brought another glint of anger to Brand's face. "That was what we counted on. If you heard rumors, you'd fire me, the old man could set me up with the Circle Four Peaks, and I'd be in a prime position to join Aiken." He laughed insouciantly. "If you'd been in on it, your loyalty would have given the whole show away when someone repeated a rumor about me."

"There were so many signs," Chantel cried. "You insisted on hanging Duke, Santa Fe. What a terrible chance you took!"

"I knew Brand wouldn't stand for any such," the foreman maintained. "Then when I volunteered to take Duke to Dillon, it was easy enough to let him slip away."

"I hated driving off your horse, Santa Fe." Regret dulled some of the twinkle in Duke's eyes. "But we had to make sure it looked authentic if we wanted it to go."

Brand looked as puzzled as Chantel felt, then asked, "How did the abduction fit in?"

"It didn't." Duke sprang to his feet. "That was a little deal of Aiken's when I was setting things up on Eagle Peak. Somehow he got suspicious of me. Chantel was his ace in the hole, as he told her, to make sure I stuck with our bargain."

"Then your building or letting those men build the Chantel saloon was all part of it? And my grandfather knew?" Chantel's brain whirled.

"It was his idea. He figured it would attract the exact kind of folks who'd fall in with Aiken."

"It might interest you to know that we've got Aiken and his men sitting in jail right now," the sheriff interjected with a smile on his heavy face. "They were only too willing to talk. They led us right to who we were really after, two of the biggest ranchers in the state who buy cattle with no questions asked." He named two names and Brand whistled. "This could be a mighty fine example for any other rustlers who might think about settling in our part of the country." He extracted himself from his chair, gripped Duke's hand with a calloused palm, and said warmly, "We've got this man to thank." His keen eyes raced to Brand. "For a whole lot." His heavy boots clumped across the floor. At the door he turned. "Want me to wire back east for that dude and his toy pistol to be picked up?"

"No." Brand shook his head. "Miss

Anita's going to have a bad enough time after eloping with him." Chantel could see the long breath he took and held before he said, "I ought to thank him."

"What for?" Santa Fe's eyes nearly popped from his head.

"If he hadn't put me flat on my back, I'd still be riding high, thinking what a great guy Brand Morgan is. I've prided myself on working hard and helping build a cattle empire. Now I know that if the Lord isn't part of it, it's not worth a thing." Unaccustomed humility struggled with his words. "When I left Virginia, I decided if there was a God or Jesus, they could stay back there. Montana Territory was far away, too far for sissy stuff like religion. She needed strong, ruthless men who'd build her up and make her a good place to live. So I did just that — only to find there's no place too remote for God's hand to reach."

His eyes sought Chantel's. "I've asked the Lord to be my senior partner from here on out." He turned to Duke, "And if this cowpuncher's willing to forgive and forget, we'll turn the Rocking M and Circle Four Peaks into a spread to be counted." He held out one hand.

Duke's face shone in the late afternoon sunlight that streamed through the shining windowpane. "Just one condition." He shook Brand's hand, and his eyes gleamed with a devilish light. "The minute you can get astride Dark Star, we'll ride over and burn the Chantel saloon."

"Agreed!" Brand's smile flashed.

"Say, where's the Triangle C come in all this planning and combining?" Santa Fe complained as Molly shooed him off toward the kitchen once the sheriff and Rosy had gone out.

"That hasn't been settled yet," Brand called after him.

Duke stood easily, his saturnine face cocked in a smirk. "I have a feeling it will be — soon." He caught up his hat and swept Chantel a low bow. "Good night, all. I don't believe my presence is required at this time."

Through his mockery, Chantel saw a wistfulness. "Good night, Duke. Thank you." Would he understand how much his friendship meant?

A flash like the path of a falling star winged its way from dark eyes to dark eyes. The next moment Duke was gone, singing a snatch from an old cowboy song.

Chantel turned from the doorway. "He did a fine thing."

"Yes." Brand looked at her through his golden lashes.

"I'm glad the rustlers and their backers have been caught."

"Yes." The corners of his mouth turned up.

She crashed blindly into his fence of monosyllables. "Is that all you can say?"

"Come here, Chantel." The same radiance that had touched his face in the little second-story room of the Circle Four Peaks ranch lighted a candle in her heart. She stumbled toward him.

"Sorry I can't get down on my knees." Two masterful hands caught her waist and lowered her to a kneeling position. "Will this do?"

She could only nod. Her treacherous heart beat like an Indian tom-tom. She could feel color coming and going in her flushed face.

"That offer is still open. The one about Dark Star and me," Brand whispered into her hair. "Only now I've more to offer you." He pulled her close, and she could hear the steady thump-thump of his heart. "With the Triangle C, we'll have a mighty fine outfit for the little wranglers and gals that may come along."

"Are you asking me to marry you?" Her voice was small, but the rush of love inside was great.

Brand's teasing stopped. With his face only inches from her own, his clear amber eyes were windows to his soul. "I love you, Chantel. More than life. Not just for what you are, but for what you've helped me to be. If you hadn't come, I would have continued bitter and empty and alone — without the presence of Jesus I tried so hard to shut out."

"I love you, Brand." The words were smothered against her lips, and the arms holding her tightened. Before she closed her eyes she saw swiftly moving storm clouds through the window and smiled. Shelter had been given. They would face whatever lay ahead — together with God.

Colleen Reece has written for numerous periodicals and is the author of over forty books, including ROMANCE READER #1 (*The Calling of Elizabeth Courtland* and *Honor Bound*). She is a creative writing instructor and is a popular speaker at writers' conferences.

Reece resides in Washington state.